THE DIARY OF A DR WHO ADDICT

Also by Paul Magrs

THE DIARY OF A DR WHO ADDICT

PAUL MAGRS

SIMON AND SCHUSTER

For Mam and Charlie

First published in Great Britain in 2010 by Simon and Schuster UK Ltd,
A CBS COMPANY

Simon & Schuster UK Ltd
1st Floor, 222 Gray's Inn Road
London WC1X 8HB

A CIP catalogue record for this book
is available from the British Library.

ISBN 978-1-84738-412-6

3 5 7 9 10 8 6 4 2

Printed by CPI Cox & Wyman, Reading, Berkshire RG1 8EX

www.simonandschuster.co.uk

CHRISTMAS HOLIDAYS, JANUARY

Late night, Saturday

Mam says that I shouldn't sit up too late talking to Jacqui. She's an old lady and needs her rest. She's had a hard time of it in recent months. She's lost her husband, and her home. She's been under a lot of stress, has Jacqui. I shouldn't pester her.

Pester her! When Mam says this, I cringe. We're all having lunch together in our country-style kitchen at the pine table. We're having gloopy red tomato soup out of rustic-style funny-shaped bowls. I open my mouth to protest, but Jacqui gets in first.

'Hey, no problem, Mary. Seriously.' She holds up her hands and gives me a swift grin. 'The kid's okay. I like talking to him. And you know me, I'm a terrible sleeper. I'm awake most nights reading.'

Mam purses her lips and goes back to cutting up hunks of her homemade bread.

'He can talk the hind legs off a donkey, though,' Mam tells my step-nanna. 'You just tell him if he's being a nuisance.'

Jacqui shrugs and winks at me through her huge tinted glasses so that Mam can't see. Then she's tucking into her lunch. The kitchen door clatters and Brian's coming in, filthy and frozen from the garden. He's sawing up old bits of wood to make a kind of runaround compound for the dog. Mam tells him to wash up before he sits down with us.

'Your mam reckons it's okay for David to sit up late talking with her.'

Brian shrugs and smiles at us both. He's got the same easy manner as his mam. He shrugs and says, 'Whatever.' He's lived in England most of his life, but his accent is still tinged a bit American, like his mam's. Even though Brian's lived with Mam and me for over a year now, I still can't get used to it. He sounds to me like someone off the telly.

'I can't understand what it is you've got to talk about, anyway,' Mam tells us, plonking the bread on the table.

What do we talk about? Jacqui and I exchange a conspiratorial glance. We talk about The Show, don't we? What else?

Mam wouldn't understand. She thinks that, at twelve – nearly thirteen! – I should be growing out of The Show by now. Mam thinks it's a daft thing. A kid's thing. Even though Jacqui's into it too. Mam thinks I should be fixing my sights on more grown-up stuff, more serious stuff. She sighs when I go on about the New Season starting on the telly, or when

I talk about the new novelisation coming out, or the monthly magazine being late arriving. She can't understand the nature of my addiction, at all.

But Jacqui can. She could see it straight away.

'Sure,' she told me later on, just before bed. 'I understand enthusiasms.' ('En-thoosiasms', she said.) 'I know about obsessions. I know what it's like to be so into something, it gets into your gut and you think about it all the time.'

Jacqui told me this while we were sitting in her bedroom. Her room at our house is more like a little bedsit. When she left the home she had shared with Brian's dad she brought some of their furniture and things with her. Most of it, however, she had to ditch, which was sad. But Mam and Brian worked hard to make her room here with us as comfortable and familiar as they could.

She brought her husband's EZ Boy reclining chair and she sits on it, dwarfed in its brown corduroy depths, as she talks into the night. I sit in my new, usual place on a footstool beside the wooden globe which houses her cocktail cabinet (you have to lift up the Northern Hemisphere on a hinge). It's in front of her tall bookcase, which goes right up to the artex ceiling and is crammed with paperback fantasy novels, all of them read and reread by Jacqui over the years.

'I guess I'm addicted to reading,' she told me, seeing where I was staring. 'It's how I get through the lonely times. There's so much of life to fill up. We've got to fix on something we like doing and make sure we enjoy it! Otherwise we're going to be pretty bored. So, I've got my reading and you've got your Show. So what? There are worse things to be fixed on at your age, believe me. You could be doing drugs or booze or glue-sniffing.'

I shrug and smile. Sometimes I still feel a bit shy of Jacqui. She seems so sophisticated. Worldly.

'Besides,' she goes on. 'I can see what you see in your Show. Of course I can. It's an escape, isn't it? Escape into another world. Other times and places.'

She stares out of the window then, through the slatted blinds that are new up. Outside it's snowing, heavier and heavier. The snow came falling down over our estate under sodium lights and it was showing no sign of stopping.

'Yeah,' she says, 'I can see why it'd be nice to go off into time and space some day with Doctor Who.'

Funny thing is, I think, she hasn't even seen a single episode yet. What she's done is read some of the books. I've lent her a couple of my novelisations in order to bring her up to speed before the New Season starts on the telly next week. She's borrowed six – no, seven – of my Doctor Who books. She seems to have enjoyed them. She gives them back to me with a strange smile. 'He's pretty neat, your Doctor Who.'

I don't have the heart to correct her: to tell her, it's the show that's called 'Doctor Who.' The Doctor is just The Doctor.

Then she asks me questions, which I'm only too happy to answer. How does he change his face? Why does he do it? And where did the Master come from? Why does he hate him? When did he meet Romana? And who was it started turning people into Cybermen in the first place?

I try to answer her as best I can. It's weird, though, a grown-up asking these questions in such a serious, intent way. Jacqui asks like the answers really matter.

No more questions tonight, though. I can see she's flagging. I remember what my mam said: Jacqui's still in mourning. Her husband's only a few months gone. She hardly knows where she's at these days. We have to be very careful with her.

I say my goodnights and she offers her cheek shyly for me to kiss. She smells of some kind of face cream and parma violets, those sickly-smelling sweets. She says she can't stand the violets either, but they're useful in helping her to give up smoking. Thing is, her dead husband's corduroy chair still smells of ciggies, just like he did.

'Sleep well, kiddo,' she tells me, like she does each night.

Jacqui never sleeps well, though. From my room I can hear her rustling about with sweet papers. I can hear her padding over to her tall bookcase. She'll be fetching down Tolkien again, probably (she says she's reread him a million times). I can hear her clambering onto the creaking chair to read away the early hours. Our bedroom doors have glass panels at the top, so that light seeps onto the hall landing. That's why, when I want to read in the night, I have to have a torch under the blankets. Mam goes mad if she thinks I'm staying up too late.

This night, just a couple of days after New Year's Eve, I'm awake wondering what the New Season will bring. I've no idea what time it is. I'm lying very still and staring at the shadows of the toys along the shelf by the bare window. I've got a few Doctor Who-type toys. Memorabilia, rather than toys, of course. The shadows thrown by the Giant Robot and the talking K9 look pretty spooky against the old wallpaper we've only half ripped down. All the while the snow's coming down, and the shadows of the flakes are scrolling down endlessly. They look like interference on a broken TV.

My head's whirring with all this stuff. At least we're still in holidays. If I'm dopey and sleepy tomorrow through lack of sleep it hardly matters. There's no school yet to worry about. I'm busy thinking about old monster enemies and hoping that some will come back. Like the Wirrn, with their huge antennae and faceted eyes and segmented bodies lumbering through space. Or the Zygons, those grotesque orange foetus-like creatures covered in suckers and able to disguise themselves as any human beings. Or the Sontarans, who were like trolls and arrived on earth in spherical ships from a distant world where everyone looked the same . . . Any of these creatures could be brought back. Part of the joy of The Show is guessing at who will come back next for a rematch with the Doctor. Every season brings some kind of wonderful return.

From my bed I can see out through the sparkling clean window at the roofs of the dark houses of Hampton Place. The streetlights are smoky orange and the night is overcast. The clouds are heavy with snow and the moonlight coming through them is a milky purple. There's the glow in the sky from the Industrial Estate. The colours of night time on this town are like the colours of Swizzels sherbet lollies.

Thick and fast the snow comes falling, thick and fast. I feel like jumping out of bed. We could take the sledge out tomorrow. I wonder if Mam and Brian would come out? And Jacqui? We could go on the hills by the Junior School, above the woods and the stream. By the looks of things, it's going to be real, proper, thick snow. Luxurious, the kind that stays. We can play out and it'll be just like 'The Seeds of Doom', when they find the deadly seed pods of the Krynoids at the South Pole. It'll be snow as thick and deep and as proper as that.

I stay awake long enough to see if it's lying. And it is, heavily and snugly, on the flat roofs of the black houses. It'll still be there in the morning. I go back to bed and fall immediately asleep, which is strange for me.

Sunday, early hours

I wake up and it's still the night. And I think: Hang on – *burglars*. There's all this noise from the kitchen below my bedroom. Not loud noise. Not, like, *noisy* noise. Just noise like someone moving about normally. Rattling the Venetian blinds that hang over the back door. They make a shivery, bladelike noise. There's the clunking of the lock. Someone's going out or coming in. And it's still that pale moonlight and the shifting snow outside.

I used to lie awake on the alert for burglars. During that time when it was just Mam and me at home. After Dad died. Before Mam met Brian in the record store where he works and they started going out. Before he moved in.

I used to expect burglars at any time. Breaking windows. Clunking about downstairs. Coming up the stairs to get us. I used to imagine what I would do. Back then I thought I had superpowers. I was just a little kid. I loved to read Marvel comics. I believed I could throw intangible force fields around people or objects, like the Invisible Girl could. I could hex

11

people with satanic bolts of light, just like Doctor Strange. I could fly and burst into vengeful flame like the Human Torch. All of that would have come in handy with burglars.

Now I've got to be brave. I can still hear the noises, now that I'm fully awake, which means they're really happening. I need to find my dressing gown and creep out into the hallway. I have to keep my cool.

I take a deep breath and cross the room, making as little noise as possible. My feet feel like lead, frozen on the rough carpet.

Out on the landing, I find Mam and Brian listening at the top of the stairs. Mam looks alarmed to see me there.

'What's happening?' I whisper.

They are both in their night things, looking scared. Mam shushes me. She gives Brian a shove, and he starts to creep down the staircase.

I tell them, 'It sounds like someone at the back door. Someone coming in the kitchen . . .' At that moment, for some reason, I look along the hallway at Jacqui's door. It's standing open. The light's off inside.

Mam jerks her head. Then she seems to burst into action. She storms down the stairs, pushing past Brian.

'In the kitchen,' she's saying. She rushes over and flings open the door. We crowd in behind her.

Sure enough, the back door is wide open. Snow that was piling up against its glass panels has tumbled onto the doormat. A freezing wind is swirling about the room, scattering cards off the swags of tinsel on the walls. The blinds are clattering and Mam is standing there, staring out into the night.

There's no sign of anyone. No burglar. No intruder. No Jacqui. But someone has been down here and they have unlocked the back door and let themselves out into the freezing night. And, judging by the small footprints in the snow in the yard, they've gone off down our street.

'My mom!' Brian gasps. 'She's walked off!'

'What?' shouts Mam.

'She used to do this, years ago. Back at home. She'd go sleepwalking at night. If she was stressed out over something.'

'Sleepwalking?' Mam says, as if she's never heard of such a thing.

'She's out there somewhere,' Brian says, looking scared suddenly. 'We gotta get after her.'

These aren't really streets. They aren't set out in straight and logical lines. Every street is a cul-de-sac and they form an intricate and complicated pattern.

Our estate seen from above would look like intestines or jungle vines or something.

In the snow it's even more confusing. It's lying thick now, melting the difference between road and path, smoothing rooftops and plastering the dog-rose hedges. Everything is being smothered. It's just past four in the morning. I can't even remember being up this late and this thought is quite exciting, even as we put on our shoes and heavy overcoats and prepare to go out and look for Jacqui. I'm in pyjamas and my dressing gown and my wellies, which still feel cold and damp inside. I've fetched my torch from beside my bed. I've set it to the strongest white beam. We're off on an adventure, it seems like. Mam wonders whether to phone the police.

'She's an old lady. She's been widowed. And you reckon she's still asleep, Brian. Look at it out there! She'll do herself a mischief!'

But we don't phone the police yet. Brian says his mother would be mortified if the police came hunting her through the streets. Mam says the police aren't much good anyway. They'd take hours to come out, no matter how serious the situation. Mam doesn't trust them and I think I understand why. My dad was a policeman. Being a policeman didn't help him much when he was hurt on duty. The back-up never got to him in time. Mam doesn't trust the coppers to do anything right, as a result. She tells Brian that we are probably better off by ourselves, hunting the streets for his mother. Jacqui can't have got far, surely. It's only been a few minutes.

In the dark garden Mam's locking up the house, stowing away the keys in the pocket of her long brown coat. And I'm shivering already. More from excitement than cold. The fences and the gate are crusted with ice that's formed overnight, since the temperature dropped right below freezing. Jacqui must have had to really wrench at the back gate to get it open. But there it is, open to the street. And there are her footprints, heading off down the path. Right onto the road. The footprints are being buried and worn away by the new falling snow. They're almost invisible already. We have to hurry.

And I am thinking, of course: *What would the Doctor do?* It's the obvious thought. The only way to be calm and self-possessed and actually do the proper thing in an adventure like this, when one of your companions' lives is at stake . . . the only correct thing is to do what the Doctor would do. And just now that means hurling ourselves into the whirling blizzard and following in Jacqui's tiny footsteps.

It's at this point that we should, by rights, hear the blood-chilling and ear-splitting roar of some kind of snow beast.

But we don't. We plough on, playing the torch beam ahead of us. Stepping gingerly on the road. The new snow has fallen on black ice that slicks the tarmac. It's treacherous. You could easily come a cropper. We are forced to slow. We call out her name into the night. It feels a bit weird to me, to be yelling out the name of an adult. But I can't really go shouting, 'Brian's Mam', can I? Or 'Mrs Goldbaum.' That would be too weird. So I'm yelling 'Jacqui', the same as Mam and Brian.

All the houses are dark around us. It's like we're alone on this whole estate. No one comes to help. And no one is even aware of us, creeping along like this, calling out. When Brian shouts, there's a quaver in his voice I haven't heard before. Usually he's so self-possessed and cool about things. I realise I've never heard him sound even mildly worried before.

Mam sounds worried so much of the time. I'm used to that edge to her voice. Quite often she sounds like this. Like she's trying hard not to give in and cry. Incredulous – that's the word I'm looking for. Mam often sounds incredulous: that something *else* bad is happening. She can't believe that something awful has happened again.

This estate we live on stretches out for a mile or two all around us, into the night. It is surrounded on three sides by the big roads, which lead to the centre and out of town, to the motorway going both north and south. That would be a bad way for Jacqui to walk in her sleep, towards the main roads. I can picture it now, her shambling along in her nightie, snow stuck in that headscarf she wears over her piled-up hair. Like a zombie, or a woman possessed by a being from beyond time and space.

This end of the estate there's all the fields of waste ground and long scrubby grass. And then it's the stark black branches of the woodland trees along the Burn. That's the name of the narrow stream running right through our town. It's been left mostly wild, like a kind of nature trail. Us kids are always playing out there, but only in the daytime. Of course you'd never go down there after dark. It has become one gigantic mass of seething, crackling, living darkness. You get the feeling that, if you crept into that dark, it would close up around you and you'd never be let out again.

'What if she's gone down there?' Mam asks Brian suddenly, seizing his arm. 'What if she's wandered off down the Burn?'

I realise that, since Jacqui has moved in with us, Mam feels responsible for her. If tonight the old lady gets lost forever, Mam will take all the blame onto herself.

'You said she's done this before?'

'Sure,' Brian says uneasily. 'She's done it, off and on, all her life. Maybe it's to do with settling into a new place. Or maybe it's something she's been reading. Something's disturbing her. I heard her say that when she was a kid she used to get up and stroll all around the neighbourhood. Cops used to bring her back. Neighbours. She was so lucky she never wound up dead. But she never went out in weather like this. Winters in New York City, you wouldn't last ten minutes in your jammies.'

Mam shoots him a look. It's like she thinks Brian isn't taking this seriously enough. But I can see that he is. He just always sounds laid-back, that's his problem. Right now that's getting on my Mam's nerves.

We're shuffling past the last few, blocky houses before the path that takes you out of our estate. This path crosses the wasteland and the abandoned boating lake, before it reaches the next estate. That's the one where we used to live, before Dad died. We moved home because Brian told Mam he thought we should have a new start. We deserved to start again and not to dwell in the past.

It's getting heavier, the snow. It's coming down in flurries and it lies like someone rolling out bolts of white, lacy material. Each flake seems to simply drop

18

and take up its position with military precision in the great mass of snow. This is an *invasion* of snow. None of it is melting or shrinking away. It feels like the snow is here to stay and, at any other time, I'd be delighted. Come the morning, me and our golden retriever, Ben, would be running about, hardly able to wait to get out to play. I'd be forcing down Ready Brek and grabbing my wellies from the cupboard under the stairs. Pulling on the woolly hat Big Nanna knitted me for Christmas. And then I'd be dashing out to be first on the fresh snow: to be the first to trample and plough it all up.

We should have brought Ben out. I wonder how good he'd be as a tracking dog. Not much use as a guard dog. He was still asleep on his blanket when we came downstairs. Ben's an elderly dog now, and he's pretty hard to wake up, even when something dramatic's going on, like tonight. He'd be glad to be out in the snow, though, I reckon. Maybe we should have brought him.

Ben's all that's left, really, of life and how it was when Dad was still around. For a while Ben seemed to be in mourning like the rest of us, and was disturbed by the change of house. He seems to quite like Jacqui, though, and sits by her in the living room at night, even though she's not that fond of dogs. Or maybe it's just upsetting to be around another dog since her own Pup died. Ben was clever enough to realise that the old lady needed someone sitting by her in the evening, and he wanted to help her settle into her new place.

Brian's had the same thought. He's talking to Mam about going back to get the dog. 'He's a tracking dog. A golden retriever!'

Mam just doesn't know. It sounds absurd to her. But we haven't had much success yet.

Nothing more is said for a bit. We are frozen and soaking. We can't stay out much longer in these conditions. It seems certain now that when we go back indoors we will have to phone somebody. The police. Official people. Someone who can sort this out. We walked out and we were vanquished by the dark. We walked to the edge of the estate, where the street lamps run out, and we came slap-bang up against the waste ground and the woodlands. If we went any further, then we would all be lost.

So we are coming back home. The new snow creaks underfoot. We can't even find the footprints we made when we set off on this expedition. We have hardly been any time at all. This is something Mam points out when she starts to speak again, in a quieter tone: 'It's only been fifteen minutes or so. She can't have gone that far. Can she?'

Brian frowns. 'I dunno. She can scoot about pretty fast when she wants to.'

What I'm imagining is an alien abduction. As we return to Hampton Place and see our house with its kitchen lights blazing in the darkness, I'm picturing what it might have been like if a saucer-shaped space craft had touched down on the waste ground in all the snow tonight. Indeed, the freak blizzard conditions might have been *caused* by that alien craft floating down through our atmosphere and settling on our estate.

It is surrounded by a glowing nimbus of unearthly light. Yes, that sounds right. And it's getting all my favourite *Doctor Who* words in, too – nimbus, unearthly. Voluminous. It is a voluminous space-craft – quite possibly dimensionally transcendental inside. And it has passed through – yes! – a calamitous rip in the very fabric of time and space. So, here it is in our little town in the North of England. The spacecraft has landed, light as a snow flake. Fleeting as a brilliant idea.

Maybe my new Nanna Jacqui knew that the spacecraft was out there. Maybe she could sense it heading earthwards. She was drawn outside, towards it, because she knew she had a rendezvous with danger and adventure tonight, at four in the morning. The sheer promise of some kind of escape drew her out of her warm bed in her bed-sitting room in our home, and it brought her to the wasteland. Jacqui approached the strange, super-heated ship. A ramp was extending down from a brilliant portal. Three extremely bizarre beings were emerging to greet her . . .

This is exactly how a new story begins. An old lady sleepwalking. Impossible snow. The arduous trek to the waste ground. The waiting gold-and-silver ship, sizzling in the frost and ice. And three alien inhabitants being weird and friendly, gathering about her. One is a squid with bejewelled tentacles; another is a genius orangutan, and the last one is composed of a fabulous crystalline substance. They explain to the lady that her help is needed. She is essential to their mission. There is something of vital importance that only she in the whole universe can do. Jacqui would accept that massive compliment with a world-weary shrug. Of course only she could be of help. Whaddizzit they want?

Nothing fazes Jacqui. Like she said to me: she's seen everything there is to see, just about.

And now the extraterrestrials are begging for her help, these outlandish and awesome figures from beyond this humdrum dimension. How polite they are – and how alluring are their interstellar plans. Jacqui is quite calm and secretly pleased to be asked.

Of course she will help them. Of course she will do the things that only she can do in order to help them accomplish their galactic mission.

All the while, of course, she is thinking of just how amazed I am going to be, when I get to hear about this. They sweep her up the shining ramp into the dome of the saucer. Then its hatch closes on her heels with a massive clang. And off whirls the space-ship. Streaking into the pale night sky over the town.

By the time we are back in our street, I'm thinking: But that must be a trick. I bet poor old Jacqui has been kidnapped by those creatures. They are probably alien mercenaries. That's the great switcheroo. The twist in the tale. Jacqui has been too keen to dash off into the cosmos. She was foolhardy. She won't be here when the Doctor comes to tell us – to tell *me*! – that he is hot on the heels of three galactic criminals, and he wants to know whether we have come across them?

When we get to our garden, I take a deep breath. Just in case. It could so easily be true, couldn't it? Just imagine there was a police box standing there, wait-ing. We could just turn the corner and there it would be. Snow already settling on its pyramid roof and glowing lamp.

There are lights on next door. We've woken up the neighbours, it seems.

The blonde twins' dad – a little man with a

beard – is coming out to greet us. He's in his wife's housecoat, pretending it's his dressing gown. 'You must be out looking for your mother, aren't you?'

Mam kicks through the snow, hurrying over to him. 'Yes!' she shrieks. 'Well, not my mother. His mother. Brian's. Why, have you seen her?' Her voice leaps out in huge relief as she gabbles.

'She's at ours,' the blonde twins' dad nods.

His wife is in the doorway of their kitchen, framed in yellow light. She's in her nightie and squinting at us. 'She came knocking at ours, the poor old thing,' she shouts. She's so much taller than her husband. 'She got lost and confused about where she belongs. Came knocking at the wrong door.'

'Sleepwalking,' Brian explains, grinning at the neighbours, all anxiety lifted. 'Hey, thanks, guys. I guess we should try locking her in her room. Or putting her in a straitjacket or some damn thing.'

The couple from next-door look at him and I just know they're not getting his sense of humour. I can see how relieved Brian is, though, that his mam – his mom – has turned out to be safe after all.

We all crowd into the neighbours' kitchen, which is quite like ours, but smells of other people's cooking. Suddenly there's Jacqui standing there in front of us, looking even smaller than she usually does. She's got one of their blankets over her thin

24

shoulders and her sopping nightie. She isn't even wearing her Jackie O tinted glasses, so no wonder she never knew where she was going. She almost looks like a kid, scared like she thinks the grown-ups are going to tell her off.

At their kitchen bench the blonde twins are wordlessly watching this scene unfold. They're my age, and in the same class as me at school. I'd expect the two of them to be pointing and laughing, but they're not. They stay quiet, drinking it all in.

'Where did you get to, mom?' Brian asks his mother as he hugs her, rubbing her arms to warm her through. 'Where did you go?'

'Nowhere,' she says when, at last, she can get her words out through her shivering. 'I woke up outside. I didn't go anywhere.' Then we see that she's holding something up. Something she's been clutching in her cold red hand.

'What's she doing with that?' Brian laughs. 'It's a whatsit, isn't it, David? One of yours?'

I look at the tiny plastic Dalek that Jacqui is holding out to show us. 'Yeah,' I say, 'It's the Dalek from the chess set.'

'What's she doing with that?' Mam asks.

Gently, she takes it out of Jacqui's hand and gives it back to me.

*

Jacqui started teaching me to play chess at the end of last year, when she moved in with us. She said, 'Hey, you're a clever kid. Did no one ever teach you to play? You gotta be able to play games.'

She has a chess set in a wooden box that folds out. The pieces are miniature and stowed away in a compartment made of foam. She says they're made of ivory. A pawn was missing and she said, 'Hey, do you have, like, toy soldiers or anything? Something we can substitute?'

I loved the way she said that. 'Substitoot.'

I dashed up to my room and hunted around in boxes, on the shelves where my old toys are kept. I picked out an inch-high Dalek from that old game, 'War of the Daleks.' I haven't played it since Robert Woolf and I took it to the woods and made a Dalek city in the mud by the Burn. There were a fair few Dalek casualties that day, with the creatures being washed away downstream. It caused a massive row between Robert and me (all sorted out now, though. It was years ago, after all.)

A gold and red Dalek would make a perfect replacement for a pawn, I decided. Then I hurried downstairs and gave it to Jacqui and she held it up to the light.

'Hey, who's this guy? A robot?'

I gasped.

Mam was on the settee, working away at her knitting. Brian was sitting by her, examining the TV guide. He'd have been thinking again how few channels we have, how little choice.

I said to Jacqui, 'But they're Daleks! Don't you know what the Daleks are?'

She smiled at me, completely baffled. I thought she was indulging me, like this was some kids' thing.

'People in America probably don't know about the Daleks,' Mam said, looking over her knitting. 'They probably don't have *Doctor Who* in New York.'

Jacqui smiled at me. 'You'll have to explain it all to me. What Daleks are. What *Doctor Who* is.'

Explain The Show to her? Was she serious?

I couldn't believe an adult was even asking. I'm always told that I talk too much about The Show. Poor Mam is completely fed up with hearing all about it. But here was Jacqui, examining the mini-Dalek and looking interested.

'It's sci-fi, yeah?' she asked, peering over her glasses. 'Like HG Wells? Like *Star Wars*?'

'A bit,' I said, and I felt stuck for words. I hardly knew where to begin.

Mam was finishing up an arm for the cardi she was making for Jacqui's Christmas. She bit the wool and cast off. 'It was first on the telly when I was David's age. And it was an old man playing the part then, in black-and-white. And the Daleks were in right from the start. We were all so scared! Everyone went mad over it, though if you see it now, it probably isn't so scary. It isn't as good nowadays as it was back then.'

Jacqui stared at her. 'You watched it too? But you don't like space things like that, Mary.'

'It's a kids' show,' Mam says. 'Everyone watched it.' She looked at Brian. 'So you never saw it, either? The Daleks and everything?'

'We had *Lost in Space* when I was a kid. *Star Trek*. I guess it was just like those shows.'

I wanted to say, 'No! No, it's nothing like any other show! It's *The* Show! It's like nothing but itself!' But I had to be polite. I've got to be welcoming. Brian's mother comes from a different culture, a different country. They have different things, different ways of doing stuff. Mam's warned me to watch out for that. And if sometimes they brag about what it's like in the States, and how everything is bigger and better and more glitzy in New York City, then we both have to bite our tongues. Brian and his mother are part of our family now. We have to be patient if they don't understand life here in the North East of England.

'*Star Trek* was great,' Brian said. 'Don't they ever show reruns of that here?'

'We used to,' Mam told him, but I know that she

hated *Star Trek*. She could never see the point in space stuff.

'We all loved *Star Trek*,' Jacqui said.

I wanted to tell them that The Show is nothing like that. Yes, sometimes it's in space and it's sci-fi, I suppose. But it really isn't like that at all.

That night, when it was bedtime, I went up and changed into my pyjamas and my new dressing gown. I brushed my teeth and came down to say goodnight to the adults. Already it had become like a ritual in our house. When I went down they were watching *Starsky and Hutch* and Jacqui was crunching her parma violets, to take her mind off wanting to smoke.

I wouldn't have minded watching *Starsky and Hutch* as well, but it was late. I wanted time enough to read before I had to put my light out. I watched them watching their grown-up show and it was true – Brian *does* look a bit like the blond one off that programme. It's all about dashing about in fast cars in New York City. Running down busy streets and alleys, dashing up and down clanking fire escapes. Brian and his mother's faces were all pale in the TV light. It was like they were drinking up the sights and sounds of NYC.

From the doorway I coughed and said goodnight, breaking their spell for a moment.

'Hey,' said Jacqui, looking ever so pleased and surprised when she saw I'd brought her a book to borrow. It was the first Doctor Who novelisation, of the very first story: *Doctor Who and the Daleks*.

It's an all-time classic. I knew how many novels Jacqui reads in a week. This seemed to be the best way of helping her to know about the Doctor and the TARDIS and everything else we take for granted. Fancy not knowing about any of it! I wished that I was reading that book for the first time.

'Oh, David,' Mam smiled. 'Jacqui doesn't want to be bothered by that. It's a kids' book . . .'

'No, no,' Jacqui waved Mam's objections away. She pointed to the pile of books she had on the coffee table she'd brought from home. 'I was going to start rereading *The Godfather* next. Maybe Doctor Who will be a pleasant change, huh?' She grinned at me and popped my book on her to-read pile with great carefulness. 'Thank you, David.'

Almost dawn

Mam's run a hot bath for Jacqui. The steam billows out on the cold landing, blue like mistfall in the early light. She doesn't want her new mother-in-law catching her death of cold, she tells her.

I pretend to sleep. The digital clock says it's nearly six. I feel fluttery and weird inside, like it's Christmas morning again. I'm supposed to be back asleep, but I'm watching the snow dropping down past the curtainless windows. It's steady and hard, filling up the world outside, and I can't shut my eyes.

At last I hear Jacqui coming out of the bathroom and back into her own bed-sitting room. The lights go out. She settles down. I can hear her through the thin wall.

Silence. And the morning light is washing into the room, a shifting blur of the palest blue. I lie on my back, staring at the purple silhouettes of the toys and annuals and stuff on the shelves. I reach for my torch and switch it on. I have a go at shining different colours up the walls, doing special effects.

I'm trying too hard to sleep. I'll give myself a headache if I try too hard. What does Mam say? Let every little bit of you relax, relax. And I ask her, isn't lying awake thinking just as restful as falling asleep? And she laughs and says, no way! You have to fall fully asleep.

But I find it so hard, with all these thoughts whirling around.

Did I really think Jacqui was lost for ever? Did I ever think she was gone for good?

I think I did. What if a real disaster had happened

here tonight? What would be happening right now, if she hadn't turned up again?

The kind of disaster like they have on the local news, when family members and neighbours come on the telly and say what a tragedy it is. And what a great person the person who disappeared always was. And how you never really expect this kind of thing to happen on your own doorstep . . .

Did I ever really think something awful had happened to Jacqui?

No.

Because that's not how these adventures work.

Things – even the worst possible things – always work themselves out in the end, I think.

Wrongs are righted. Invasions are foiled. Time bombs defused. Time is run backwards. Everything is saved. Danger becomes something you can laugh at.

Evil is vanquished.

If only you can keep your head, and stay brave and you never give in.

That's what I think, lying here awake in the snow.

Monday

The weather is going to get worse and worse. All the adults mutter about it. They are saying it on the local news, and in the paper Brian brings home with him from work in the shop.

We could get snowed in. That's what everyone is saying. The whole of our little town, surrounded by fields, miles from anywhere. It would be so easy, if the snow just kept up, for us to be lost and trapped here.

I don't mind. I don't know what the adults are on about. What's so wrong with being snowed in? We would just have to stock up with provisions. Make sure we had enough woolly blankets and library books. It would be OK. School term starts again next week, and perhaps the snow will interfere with that. That would be the best thing.

Spaghetti hoops, tomato soup, sliced white bread, margarine, Cobanas and Topics, Crunchies and Glees, Tudor crisps in family-sized assortments, cherry bakewell tarts, baked beans, oven chips, beefburgers, fishfingers, meat pies, sliced ham, tinned peaches, custard.

We should be stocking up our cupboards. For 'in the event'. Like a nuclear war. Like fall-out. In science fiction it almost sounds cosy. The hiding underground and eating all your favourite food. Having singalongs to drown out the worst of the noise from the nuclear winter above. And coming out months later to discover the world wiped clean. Finding radioactive mutants patrolling the wasteland. Quite good! Better than round here, where there's never much excitement on the whole. And Woodham Comp would be levelled. Woodham Comp would have ceased to exist. Just snow everywhere and starting again with a handful of survivors in the remains of Newton Aycliffe.

Mam mutters darkly about the weather when me and her make our way to the town centre for shopping on the Monday after Jacqui's sleepwalking stunt. We're tiredly pushing along through the snow and Mam's gazing into the sky. The snow is on pause. Suspended up there like freeze-frame on the video. The whole sky creaks and groans with weight. It's a dense, unhappy shade of grey. The grey of nothing on the telly.

When we're in the town precinct Mam is stopped

by a few people she knows – other adults muttering about the weather and casting glances at the troubled sky. She doesn't stop to talk with them for long. Besides, it's hard to make out what people are saying, they're all so muffled up in scarves and hats and collars pulled up. The steam shunts out of them like everyone's smoking fags.

Mam doesn't want to hang around too long down the town centre. That's a shame, because I love our wonderful futuristic precinct, with its two levels and concrete pedestrian ramps and spiral staircases. This place has nearly all the shops you'll ever want. My favourite place is Stevens, where they sometimes have *Doctor Who* books. But I know I won't be getting anything today, after our trip on Saturday to Darlington.

This precinct is a two-mile walk from our estate: over the Burn and through the older, nineteen-fifties part of town, where the gardens have hedges round them and the houses have chimneys. On the way back, Mam is staring at the snow heaped and blanketing the pointed rooftops and the way the roads are frozen and stuck with snow. 'Where will it all go?' she says. 'It won't melt away. It'll just keep on building up and up. Will we all get buried?'

I imagine us turning into some kind of lost town. A Neolithic tribe of people preserved in ice for future generations to dig up and examine. 'This,' they'll say, 'is how it was, back in the nineteen-eighties. Look at the funny little people in the dinky little town.' We'll be like some modernistic Pompeii or something, and maybe that would be all right.

I'm stewing all this over as we trek home again with carrier bags, and Mam pulling Jacqui's bag-on-wheels. Mam hates the bag-on-wheels, thinking it makes her look like an old lady, when she's only twenty-nine. But it makes things easy as we shush and shuffle our way through the unmelting snow, up and down hills, back to our estate.

Lunch is sausage rolls from the bakery. They're still a little warm in the greasy paper bags. Mam dishes up some vegetable soup she's made and we listen to Radio One in the kitchen. Mam likes music on all the time. She likes pop, loud and brash. It fills up the time and the quiet, she says. Stops you thinking about stuff too much. And as we sit there it's almost like it's getting dark outside over our estate. The snow is starting to spiral down again. We missed getting caught in it, but there'll be a heavy fall this afternoon. I'm keen to get out in it. To be there when it falls.

'You'd better wrap up,' Mam says. 'And don't stay out too long. You'll get pneumonia, or something.'

*

Up in my bedroom I'm putting on extra socks. I'm checking if my gloves have dried – scratchy and crunchy – on the radiator. Through the curtainless windows I can see how thick and freely the snow is falling now. It looks fantastic. Twilight in the middle of the day. I catch my breath and think: if ever magical or weird stuff was going to happen in my life, it should be on an afternoon like this one. And I can't sit around indoors waiting for it to happen. I need to get out into the snow.

As I get myself ready to face the elements I put on a record, my favourite, dead loud. Geoff Love's *Space Themes* LP. A vast orchestra bashing out the theme from *Doctor Who*. After a few booming, spooky bars Mam is yelling up the landing. She's got a migraine coming on. She could do without that racket. All the whirling flakes and the worry about snow have triggered a migraine like fireworks in her head. She will have to lie in a dark room all afternoon. I turn down the sound on the Geoff Love album.

I give a little knock at Jacqui's door to say hello and find her swaddled up with her books for the afternoon. She's reading a thick novel called *Children of Dune* which she says is very complicated but she has to read it as it's the final book in the trilogy. She's frowning with concentration and crunching those flowery-smelling sweets. She gives me a kind of distracted wave from the depths of her chair.

But me: I'm going out. I hurry downstairs with my keys (I'm very proud of having my own house keys. Mam had them cut for my last birthday, when I was twelve). For a moment I think about taking out the dog for a walk. He looks a bit tired though, flumped on his blanky in the kitchen. He gives a kind of snort when I scratch his ears and ask him if he wants to come out.

My wellies are still clodded with snow, drying out on the newspaper sheets in the downstairs hall. I squeeze back into them with my thick socks on, and when I get outside they're still not on right. I'm standing in them like they're weird high heels and my coat's hanging off and my scarf's flying up as I bang the front door shut.

Monday afternoon

Robert Woolf is still my friend.

We've been best friends since we were nine and he moved to our town. Then, last year, when we went into Woodham Comp, things changed because he was put into a different class to me. For a while it seemed like we would have to have new friends and hang about with different people. But it's OK. We're still friends.

Even if he did betray me on the first day of the Comp.

But I'm not thinking about that now. I'm wading through the crust of snow, out of Hampton Place, over the twisty main road, through the gully by the flats and the play park with the metal snail thing, and into Brackett Close, where he lives in the middle of a terrace.

He opens their back door and he's wearing just blue tracksuit bottoms and his straight fair hair is standing on end. 'What is it?' He looks at me and laughs because I'm all togged up in my big coat and scarf and wellies. He's just got out of bed, I think. He's drinking cold milk straight out of the bottle and this seems scandalous.

I step into his kitchen and see at once that the place is a tip. There are foil trays and things left over from a takeaway, dripping with yellow gravy. The place smells of stale Chinese food and fag ash. The blinds are still drawn against the sky, premature against the day's fading. The house seems unaired and disordered. From somewhere upstairs there comes the sound of a David Bowie record: all weird distortions and his nasal, plaintive singing. Robert's glamorous older sister must be up there, playing her records and putting on her elaborate make-up. Sitting in front of her mirror and piling up her white-blonde hair as she sings along with Bowie.

Both the Woolfs are glamorous to me. Even though their house smells of last night's Chinese and fag ash and my mam would go spare if she could see the mess round their house. They seem glamorous to me because they do just what they want. Their mother works in Fine Fare, taking as much overtime as she can to support them. She's on shelf-stacking duties through the night and often sleeps in the day. She must be a pretty heavy sleeper, what with all the music going on round theirs. Robert reckons she's got a new fella on the go, too, and more often than not she's round at his flat on the next estate. With all this going on her teenage daughter is usually in charge of her house and brother. And so Robert and his sister get to do stuff that they want to with no grown-up interference. It seems fantastic to me, unreal. Alison is in a punk band and sometimes they rehearse in the living room. I've been round once while they did so. They all act so casual, as if everyone round here is in a band, or paints murals on their council house walls, or plays their records as loud as they like.

I sit at the kitchen table in the dim room and

watch Robert put the kettle on. I watch his long pale back in the slatted light through the blinds. It's white and pink, with the impression of his crumpled sheets still printed, and he's got a sprinkling of pink spots. Even his spots seem like evidence of greater maturity. Certainly his making tea for us both does. It's only recently that Mam has let me use the kettle, for fear of me having a terrible accident and scalding myself. She thinks I'm completely incompetent and a danger to myself, so hot-drink-making – at twelve – is still novel to me.

'Do you think school will actually start next week?' I ask Robert.

He shrugs. 'Why shouldn't it? Because of the snow?' He looks nonplussed. 'That won't stop them. We'll still have to be there. Doing rubbish lessons. Studying irrelevant stuff.'

Robert is an anarchist. He read something about being one in the *NME* and now he gets cross about most things we have to do, especially at school. I find the whole anarchist thing interesting, but quite hard to get a grip on. The idea of no rules at all makes me feel a bit unsteady.

'It's snowing again,' I tell him, nodding towards outside, though he's already seen that. In the few moments the door was open a heap of snowflakes tumbled into the kitchen. They have only just melted away there. And then I remember I haven't told him the tale of our Saturday night and how my new step-nanna Jacqui wandered off, asleep, across the estate.

We drink our tea out of mugs at the table and he listens with interest, nodding every now and then, and flicking through *Smash Hits*. 'Look at this lot of posers in here,' he sneers, as he studies pictures of some New Romantic band. 'That's not real music. That's not art.'

I sigh. He's always on about what's 'real' music or 'real' art, is Robert. He hates anything showy or fake or commercial. Him and his sister, both. They see it as a political thing. They don't want to have anything to do with what they call 'the mainstream'. And they've explained to me that that means anything ordinary and normal. They want nothing to do with the kind of things that ordinary people like.

'We only love esoteric things,' was what Alison once said to me. It was the only time she ever addressed me directly. She was in a kind of silver wrap she had made herself and her white hair was standing on end with sugar-water. Her make-up was just like Bowie's on the cover of his album, *Aladdin Sane* – a large blue lightning bolt across her face. There was a whole bunch of her older, punky friends round the house, smoking and drinking cans on a Saturday afternoon. And, in this very kitchen, Alison turned to me – to me! – and said, 'We only love esoteric things. Do you know what that means?'

And I didn't. I still don't. But it sounds fantastic. I only want to love esoteric things, too.

Alison smelled of patchouli oil and white musk incense. There's a shop in Darlington called Guru that smells just the same way. It seems to stand for a whole world of weirdness and things that are . . . well, esoteric. It's as if this house of theirs isn't really on our estate, after all. It stands at the portal of another world. Not our town any more, but a dimension where everything is esoteric.

Then I say to Robert, who is blowing on his tea, 'The Show is on tomorrow. The start of the new season.'

'Oh, really?' he says. Feigning nonchalance. I just know it. He'll have the *Radio Times*, same as me. He'll have a sixty-minute audio cassette ready, same as me, so he can tape the soundtrack of the episode as it is broadcast. He'll have his tape recorder jammed up against the telly speakers. He'll be as excited as I am about it.

'The new Doctor,' I tell him, urging him to comment. Urging him to show his keenness. A little tingle goes right through me, now that I'm talking about it. The very idea of Peter Davison walking about, talking and acting as the new Doctor, and putting on his new outfit of cricketing whites, and being the Doctor and having a new adventure – and that being just over a day away . . . it makes me feel tingly now. I slurp my tea.

Robert looks at me and I can see a sneer start to form. He's got a friendly face, with a wide mouth and expressive features. You can see plainly what he's thinking, and this is one of the things I like about him. But now he's putting a superior sneer on. How can he? How can he sneer about The Show?

'Y'know,' he says. 'Sometimes I wonder if we're getting too old for it.'

'What?' I can't believe what I'm hearing. 'For The Show?' The breath catches in my throat.

He nods, and I can see he's just about laughing at my reaction. But then he looks thoughtful. 'Yeah. I do. Don't you ever? I reckon that maybe I should have outgrown it. It's kids' stuff. Fantasy.'

But . . . this is like heresy! I stare at him. I put down my Kitkat mug. The tea was horrible anyway, too weak, with sticky sugar on the handle.

'Our Alison says that it's you – you're obsessed with The Show, Davey,' Robert Woolf tells me, scratching himself. 'She says it's a bit pathetic. A bit

44

rubbish. So I'm thinking that maybe I shouldn't be so into it any more. I should start thinking about growing out of it. I shouldn't really care about it any more.'

Now I'm gawping at him. Then he says, 'But I'm still going to watch the new season start.'

Robert has got the smallest bedroom in their house. His bed is a mattress on the floor, and his record player is on the floor, too, right next to it, so he doesn't have to get out of bed to change his records. He's got a set of free weights and a heap of vinyl LPs, and that's almost all there is in his room. I'm sitting on the end of his mattress, listening to a record he's insisted I need to listen to, and I'm thinking that my own room feels like a little kid's room in comparison. My room is all toys and kids' stuff.

The record is some Goth thing that his sister recommended to him. Bells are clanging, there's lots of discordant, scraping guitar noise, and someone is chanting ominously in the background. I try to read the sleeve, to see what the song titles are, but there aren't any.

'It's just one long piece of music,' Robert tells me, lifting one of his weights. 'They went to a castle in Ireland and lived there for six months in the dark. They recorded this all as one piece. That's real art and dedication. None of your commercial rubbish. That's proper music.'

I watch him as he sits back up on his mattress, leaning against the far wall. He hefts his weights and listens very carefully to the awful record. He's starting to get proper muscles, I realise. His chest is looking firmer, broader. I look away, embarrassed, but he's so lost in his Goth record he doesn't even notice me stare for a second or two.

'Don't you think it's fantastic?' he shouts over the racket.

I nod, smiling enthusiastically. I think about Mam playing Radio One in our kitchen. I think of all the big, popular songs of this year, and hearing them in the morning before heading out to school. Mam likes everything that's in the charts – most things, at any rate. We all do, in our house. We make tapes to play in the car from the *Top Twenty* of Sunday night. We buy singles and albums and usually it's bright, jangly, commercial pop that we get. Round our house, Blondie is probably the most alternative and punky that we get.

Round Robert's house music seems such a solemn, difficult thing. You have to be very serious to listen to it properly. You have to sit tangled up in stale sheets, listening very carefully to loud music.

There's banks of dust on the carpet. There's an

unaired feeling to these rooms, blue like the mould floating in the coffee mug by his mattress. But it feels exciting just being here. It makes me feel artistic. What's the word Robert kept using for weeks on end earlier this year? His sister had taught him it.

Bohemian. That was it. Living in a mucky house. Listening to loud, tuneless records. It's being bohemian. It's being punk. Even after everyone else has sold out and gone ordinary.

I sit there on his sheets and I feel thrilled. I'm being bohemian, just by being here.

There's a knock at the door we can hardly hear over the noise. His sister Alison pokes her head in. She looks beautiful. She's painted her face bone white. She's got a cupid's bow mouth in fuschia lipstick. A beauty spot and clown-like eyes under her bleached hair. She looks like the pierrot clown on the front of Bowie's *Scary Monsters* LP. 'Robert!' she shouts at him, glancing at me briefly. 'I'm off out. We're rehearsing in Darlington . . .'

Robert turns the sound down on his record. Secretly I'm pleased. As we both look up at the vision in the doorway – she's in black-and-yellow waspy striped leggings and a fluffy red jacket – I feel very self-conscious in the chunky knit sweater my mam knitted me. My blue cords that are a bit flared. But Alison takes no notice of me.

47

'I might not get back tonight, if the weather keeps up,' Alison warns him. 'Mam won't be in either. You'll be OK on your own, won't you?'

'Course,' he says, curling his weights vigorously. 'Course I will.'

I realise Alison looks excited and keen to be gone. 'We're going to record the whole of the album in one long session. We're going for the whole thing.'

We gaze at her in admiration. Alison sings backing vocals and plays the violin for Titus Groans. I've heard them a couple of times round here, and on tape, and they are fantastic. They are weird and I don't quite understand what they do – they are another band without tunes, and without endings to their songs – but I think what they do is somehow magical.

'What's your little friend around for?' she asks him.

Robert shrugs. 'He just came round.'

Alison shrugs back and pulls a face at us. Then she is gone, clopping down the carpetless hall stairs in her Doc Martens. *Little friend.* I hate that.

Robert turns the sound up on his record again, but not so loud as before. He sighs as the back door slams. Now he's left alone in his house. I can't believe it. I couldn't imagine being left alone like that. What's going to happen to him? Will he make himself something to eat? I could imagine having a go with the cooker and oven chips or something, and burning the house down. But Robert's not like me. He's confident. I ask him if he wants to come to ours. We could put him up overnight, maybe – we could find the room. He looks at me incredulously.

'I'm happy here,' he says. He picks up a black paperback from where it lies splayed beside his bed. It's the novel of *The Exorcist*.

I start telling him about the *Doctor Who* books I got in WH Smiths on Saturday. He pulls a face and looks massively unimpressed. I ask him, 'Can I borrow your *Day of the Daleks* and *The Auton Invasion*?' These are two third Doctor novels by Terrance Dicks that Robert has and I don't. I've read them before already, but they are two of my favourites.

He nods towards the wardrobe. 'They're in there.'

The tangled-up clothes – all black – in his wardrobe make me feel sad. His stuff looks like it's just been chucked in there. But his having a wardrobe seems like a grown-up thing, too. All my clothes are neatly folded by Mam into the airing cupboard on the landing.

There is a pile of paperbacks at the very back of his wardrobe. I flick through *The Omen*, *The Stand*, *Carrie*, *The Fog* and find his small stash of Target

Terrance Dicks books. There's a fat novel there called *The Fan Club* with a naked woman on the front.

He laughs. 'Hey, I'll have to lend you that one sometime. You might learn something.'

I hope he doesn't insist on lending it to me today. What would I do if I had to smuggle a dirty paperback into our house? Mam would be sure to find it. What would I say? And Robert would think I was soft, or not interested, if I said I didn't want it. But luckily he doesn't press the point. I find the *Dalek* and the *Auton* books and clutch them to me. Time to go. I don't want to hang around in this musky, dusky house all day. The point was to get out into the snow. It doesn't seem as if Robert wants to go anywhere today. He's happy lying about and lifting weights and listening to his hellish records.

'Pass me that exercise book,' he tells me. There's a blue-covered book nicked from school lying amongst his stuff.

'Are you writing a story?'

'Nah,' he says. 'It doesn't belong to me.'

I flick through. Most pages are covered in tight handwriting. There's about four different people writing this, you can tell. It's one continuous story, written in chapters.

'You know that lass, Karen, in our class? And Helen, her mate?'

I nod. They are part of Robert's new gang. They can all be quite exclusive together, in Class 1M. But Karen is always nice to me. Chatty and friendly.

'Well, they're writing this novel together, with two other girls.'

'A novel! What about? And why have you got it?'

'Karen lent me it. She sent me it in the post before Christmas. The others don't know.'

Before I pass it to him my eye catches a few phrases: *Helen moved over to Simon Le Bon now and she was sitting on his knee, kissing him* . . . and something about '*her melon-like breasts*'. I feel myself blush. 'They're writing rude stories together?'

He grins. 'All about them themselves, being on holiday on a tropical island with Duran Duran and The Cure! It's hysterical!'

I don't think he should be reading it. It feels too private. I wonder why Karen even sent it to him. She was asking to be mocked by doing that. He'll have her life.

Melon-like breasts . . . !

I think about some of the fantasy stories I've written, and I've ripped them up pretty smartish afterwards. I would die if anyone ever found them. But here's Karen – I can picture her now: purple hair, pink blusher, rather quiet and kind-looking. Here she is sending her writings in the post to him. But why?

He's holding the exercise book so carefully. Like it's rare. Like it's an unearthed treasure from *The Pyramids of Mars*.

Later, Monday afternoon

My socks have slipped down inside my wellies. I didn't want to mess about, back at Robert's house, sorting them out. So when I step out again, trudging through the snow, my heels are bare inside my boots. I could go home now, seeing as Robert's not coming out to play. It's darker still and the heavier snow is starting in earnest. But I don't want to go back yet. I'm enjoying being out by myself. I head for the Burn.

The new snow is powdery and dry as it lies on the old, frozen stuff. It makes the hill at the back of Robert's terrace very slippery and sheer. There are scraps of black bin bags lying abandoned. Kids must have been out sledging on them.

The Burn's black mass of trees looks even denser with the snow swirling round. The sky has gone orange, streaked with banners of purple. It's amazing, when you look for all the colours, in a scene that should be mostly black-and-white. Even stark and bare, the trees are a woody green and rusty brown. The snow is all shades of blue, almost silver in places. The trodden-on snow is fudgey like soft brown sugar.

Down the deep dip of Burn Lane, cars are inching slowly towards the town centre. Already the sodium yellow lights are on, making everything look two-dimensional. I keep on walking. I want to see the Burn. I love the way the stream tries so hard to freeze over. It gets all these flimsy, brittle sheets of ice forming from either side and it's as if they are straining to meet in the middle. The ice is keen to trap the running water beneath, to seal it away from the elements.

I stop at the bridge to stare down and the water is bronzey and bloody and still moving through the rocks and shaggy algae. The banks are heaped with snow and weird little petrified icicles hang down like the teeth of combs. Beyond this bridge is the concrete bridge under Burn Lane, smelling of wee and echoing with traffic rumbles and daubed with the most extravagant graffiti. Beyond that the Burn continues wending all the way out of town. I followed it that way last summer, on a walk alongside the stream with my Big Nanna. She was teaching me the names of the trees (silver birch, horse chestnut, sycamore) and the calls of the birds (cuckoo, wood pigeon, starling).

There aren't many birds to hear today. Everything is muffled by the snow. All I can really hear is the grind and shuffle and buzz of the traffic overhead, and then the river sounds echoing under the concrete bridge as I hurry underneath. Sewer-like sounds. I think about when I snuck a read of James Herbert's *The Rats*. It was Brian's copy, on the wall unit in the living room. The first proper grown-up book I have read. It stopped me coming down here, down by the Burn, for some weeks. If the rats came to take over the world, eat everyone and so on, it's from just such a place they would start out. The lopped-off tunnel mouths of sewers, like the one under the concrete bridge.

I still don't like lingering here. I hurry through, and back into the snow. Out this way the Burn is wilder. The footpath alongside it is more overgrown, with tall grasses and unruly bushes squeezing it narrow in places.

There are no council estates on this side of Burn Lane. This is where they are starting to build private houses. Posh houses. A bit further on, a mile in this direction, there is another bridge and a steep climb, and then you get to the edge of Woodham Comp's playing fields. This is the way I walk to school now, and have been doing since I started there, last September.

This is my walk to school. Why am I doing it now, right in the middle of the holidays?

Maybe to see how different it is, all snowed in. I'm struggling through deep, untouched snow here, tough and crusty as meringue. No one has been here to mess about in it. Stiff spears of tall yellow reeds and rushes stick through the snow, glittering in what's left of the light. There's a strange dusty smell of fresh snow. Ozoney. And a tinge of woodsmoke from somewhere and, for a fleeting moment, I hope it's our school burning down, up on that hill.

Woodham Comp has been lying quiet, still, unlit, since the last day of term before Christmas. That was the first day of snow we had, I realise now. Two weeks ago, when the snow started falling and we didn't see it at first, not until it had layered a clean ground coat on everything. Our whole school was assembled that afternoon in the main hall, watching a giant film screen. They were showing *Superman* for everyone as an end-of-term treat. It was only towards the end that people started noticing the snow, through the gaps in the tall velvet curtains at one side of the hall.

We'd all seen *Superman* before. It was years old. But we loved seeing it again, crackling on that big screen. We loved the way it was a secret until it started. Until then we had thought it was going to be an army recruitment film again. A cheer went up when the music first started and, for that afternoon at least, those teachers who had seemed so strict and awful during the first term of Woodham Comp, were now almost kindly.

When we came out of school that tea-time it was into a Swizzels lolly purple and orange dusk. We ran into the thickly-drifted fields, ploughing headlong across the covered-up football fields. We were singing the *Superman* theme and pretending that we were flying. All of us were doing it, that was the funny thing. And no one laughed at anyone else for pretending to be superheroes. It was as if that was OK at Christmas in the Comp. So we were all doing the same thing and everyone fitted in for once: even the weedy kids, the fat kids, the smelly kids, and the kids who get called puffs.

But today I carry on walking past Woodham Comp. Even past the hills where they make us run cross-country. I always come in last, thinking I can taste blood, lungs heaving, legs shaking, electing to walk right at the back. Even when our PE teacher is jogging alongside and screaming in my face.

I carry on, and the stream gets ever narrower and it's so thin it's coated with ice. But you can still see it alive and silvery, running beneath the surface.

This is the very edge of town. It's where it stops

being our town and turns into countryside and that goes on, uninterrupted for mile upon mile, all around County Durham. I'm struggling along as the wind and snow bend to face me and now I'm even wearing the balaclava my Big Nanna knitted me. It was bundled up in my pocket. I think about the picture of Mole in the snow in *The Wind in the Willows*. That's what I look like. I just know it. But there's no one here to see.

I'm almost at the motorway. The A167 to Darlington, where the buses go. The thunder of that traffic is just as fierce as ever. The snow isn't holding up the big traffic. So I guess Alison will have made it OK to her band rehearsal. Maybe she's already there by now. Playing her violin and helping Titus Groans to record their 'concept album', as Robert describes it.

She smelled of some kind of spicy talcum powder when I saw her this afternoon. I'd never smelled that scent before. It was probably something she had bought in one of the tiny hippy shops in the back streets of Darlington. I can conjure that smell now and it is silvery and black like the churning, endless snow.

As I get right up to the edge of town it's as if all the details are blurring and blanking out. There's nothing but the whiteness. At the edge of Newton

Aycliffe, perhaps, there is nothing else. The very world stops at the A167. Everyone who's here now is sealed inside for ever. Newton Aycliffe is closed off. Going nowhere ever again.

I don't know if it's a cosy thought, or an awful one. But I can see how it happens. The traffic noise dulls. The details are bleached out of the landscape. There's a great area of misty nothingness surrounding us like a protective quilt.

Alison got out, onto her bus to rehearsals, but maybe she'll never get back through the snow.

In The Show last year they had a similar phenomenon. A dimension that was all white and featureless. A world of just nothing. E-space, it was called. Empty space. And that's what's all around us and our town today. I've seen it with my own eyes. I had to come here, right to the edge, to see.

We're not going anywhere.

Monday night

I've been reading all night. I've been reading under the tent of my blankets with my torch. *The Auton Invasion*, and then *The Day of the Daleks*.

In the second book there's a chapter where the

Doctor holds a vigil in an empty house, waiting for the monsters to come and get him. He sips wine and nibbles biscuits as soldiers patrol the grounds and his assistant Jo Grant grows nervous. It's the perfect thing to be reading at three a.m. Just knowing that he's about to be attacked and drawn into an adventure in the far future with the Daleks. And even though I know exactly what's going to happen, I'm still turning pages, skimming through the words, cramp in my hand from holding the torch steady . . . and then I hear the noise downstairs.

I get up. I bring the torch with me. I have to investigate. Could it be Jacqui again?

I'm not even sure if I'm scared as I go down the stairs. I'm still inside the story. I feel swimmy and weird, but not really scared.

When I get down to the kitchen, Mam's doing the ironing. There are great heaps of clothes lying tangled on the pine table, spilling out of yellow laundry baskets. She's in a world of her own, pressing and steaming; folding and turning and shaking out T-shirts, uncrumpling sleeves. The only light comes from the street lamp beyond the garden fence, slatted by the blinds and made spectral by snow. I can't believe she's ironing in the dark. Monday night is Mam's turn to be the insomniac.

The insomniac. It sounds like a monster. The beast inside somebody's head. Possessing them and controlling their thoughts and actions. The Insomniac would have glittering, faceted eyes like a fly and a chitinous hide of green and black. It would sit on a high throne and mutter things inside your skull. Terrible, paranoid thoughts that only you could hear.

'Mam . . . ?' I call, as I step into the kitchen. She just about jumps out of her skin.

'What are you doing up?' she says, cross at being disturbed. She holds the iron upright and it disgorges a sharp hiss of steam. Her new iron. The one she had before wasn't a steam one.

'The noise woke me up,' I lie. And then I see what she's so busy ironing. School shirts, crisp and white. School trousers and PE kit. Everything is laid out just so. Everything is just about ready. The sight of these hated garments, still stiff and newish after one term, makes me feel sickly. It'll soon be time to go back.

And then I realise the other thing she's been doing in the night. The swags of tinsel and the Christmas cards are gone. They're stowed in a box by the door. And, if I went down the hall to the front room, I suppose I'd see that the Christmas tree was down. The decorations packed away, the stiff little arms of the artificial pine folded up. Everything ready to go back into the cupboard under the stairs. Christmas is finished. Everything's gone away. That's what Mam has decided tonight. Enough of the holidays now. In an exact reversal of Christmas Eve . . . we'll wake tomorrow and it'll be ordinary again.

She gets these fits on her. She never waits till January the sixth and the real end of Christmas. After New Year the Christmas stuff depresses her and it all has to come down. Whereas I like to eke it out. Christmas isn't over till you've had the last of your Christmas sweets, that's what *I* think.

'You can't stay up all night, doing that,' I say to her.

The table is filled with my clothes, and hers and Brian's. She could carry on for hours if she wanted. She could make it last till morning. She blinks at me like I've said something silly. Why shouldn't she stay up all night and do all of this? Who is there to stop her? It's her own house, with her rules. Better to spend time doing something useful like this – so she can send us all out into the world neat and smart – than lying down and trying too hard to fall asleep.

She doesn't even have to say any of that to me. I know she can't sleep, and she'd rather be making use of the time.

The snow has started up again outside. I watch Mam swooshing hot steam on a crumpled white shirt. She works energetically, filling the room with warm, soapy fragrance. It's as if she could melt the snow with her effort. Sizzle it away to nothing. I shiver, and remember the feeling of E-space at the town's edge.

I do as I'm told and go back up to bed. Knowing that the Christmas stuff is gone now, and that Mam is warming the kitchen ready for breakfast. Kindling the heart of the house in the coldest part of the night. And making me neat for school starting again.

'Good night, pet,' she calls after me as I set off back up the stairs. And there's a squirming excitement in the pit of my stomach as I remind myself that tomorrow's as good as Christmas Day anyway. At least, it is to me. It's the day that the first episode of the new season is on. It's what I've been waiting for. And not even the thought of those bits of clean uniform can spoil that glimmer of anticipation.

And I sleep soundly now till morning. I wake to hear Brian leaving for work, the back door banging hard on his heels.

I go downstairs for porridge and toast and find all the ironing sitting in baskets, waiting to go up to the airing cupboard. It looks immaculate and impossible, like something the fairies have been up to while I was pretending to sleep.

*

Last term, Mam taught me to tie my tie for Wood-ham Comp. It took hours, what with me being left-handed and doing it in the mirror. The tie is black-and-white and bottle-green stripes and Mam was a bit tearful when she saw me in it. It was too tight: I realised that on the first day. The idea at Woodham Comp among the kids is to do them as loose as possible, with the wide bit shorter than the narrow. I'd seen them in town on their lunch break – the cool kids from Woodham Comp, eating cones of chips and wearing their ties fat.

For a number of weeks before I began the Comp, my new uniform waited in boxes, in cellophane wrappings all summer, fresh from the catalogue. I had underpants, seven pairs, with the days of the week and suitable drawings on the front (Saturdays were in orange trim and someone kicking a football on the front). Mam bought iron-on tags with my name printed a hundred times over. I had them on everything, even the insides of my knee-length socks, and the ends curled up after a couple of washes, scratching like mad. I had a black blazer with the school badge sewn on the breast pocket, bought at huge expense. I wore it the first week at the Comp, saw that no one else ever does, and I've never worn it again. What everyone does wear is the V-necked bottle-green jumpers – the ones that stretch out of all shape. Everyone's is the same. It became a kind of trend for us in the autumn term, an aspiration: your jumper hanging right down, the sleeves past your fingers. You could tell the brand-new kids: they were conspicuous in their jumper-shaped jumpers.

Here, in the Christmas holidays, I know I am safe, but seeing the uniform all ironed like that and ready makes me feel sick. Being sick is what I do on Sunday nights, Monday mornings, when school dread is coming on. When I am putting on a white shirt with the stiff, paper collar sewn in. When I am picking clods of grassy mud off my football boots' studs and packing my tupperware box of sandwiches in my sports bag.

The thing about the Comp is that it's too big. It's dirty and messy. Even though you have to dress up to go there, it's filthy and drab. And nobody knows who you are. It seems that the people who get noticed are the mouthy ones, the badly-behaved ones. Those who would have been labelled naughty in Woodham Juniors are the ones who seem to rule this school.

Back in Woodham Juniors we were the oldest ones. We were sophisticated and we studied very advanced topics such as Birds and Wildlife, and

Roman Britain. Here we are just the kids again, and the teachers talk to us like we're daft. There's a horrible smell, too, of custard skins and greasy mince; unwashed hair and B.O. It never smelled like that in the Juniors. Not in Ms Finch's class. She put sweet-scented freesias in jam jars around the low windowsills. Her classroom smelled of chalk dust, wax crayons and the woody scent of fresh new drawing paper.

Ms Finch treated us like real people. She was funny and sarcastic. Sometimes all she had to do was raise her eyebrow at the right moment and that could have the whole class bursting out laughing. She was very fond of double-meanings, often quite rude ones. She was very thin, pale and elegant and she wore stylish outfits like Princess Diana, with ruffly collars on her blouses and tailored skirts. Sometimes she was ill with her nerves. That's what the headmaster said, when he came to stand in for her. And that made me feel closer to Ms Finch too, because sometimes Mam is very ill with her nerves. She puts it in the same language. When Mam is bad like that she'll stay in her darkened bedroom all day and we'll take her china cups of hot lemon, being careful not to let the saucer clatter noisily when we set it down.

Sometimes I consider using 'bad with nerves' as

an excuse to get out of PE. Would Mam write me a note? *David can't go dashing about in all that freezing mud today, getting rained on and jeered at. He's bad with his nerves today.* Or maybe it's something only women get. I don't know.

Since I've been at the Comp I've been feeling like I've come to the wrong place. Back in Ms Finch's sunny, glass-walled classroom I was painting water-colour pictures of birds and wildflowers. I was writing stories and she told me they could go on for as many pages as I wanted. Now I'm doing things like metal-work and standing in what they call the 'machine shop', and the teacher is telling us, 'Now don't be intimidated by the machines, lads. Because let's face it, these are the things you may well be using every day at your work in the future.' They've got drills and furnaces and brazing hearths and lathes. Everything spins blades or shoots out flames. Everything vibrates and judders and screeches. It smells of sulphur and acid and the blood-like tang of molten metal. I can't believe they let the rough kids in our class loose on those machines, heating things up till they go white hot.

I hung back and avoided using the machines. I filed down the key ring I was supposed to be making and, over the autumn term, it got smaller until there was hardly anything left. No one else thought it was weird, that the teacher was saying we'd most likely be working in a factory with machines when we went into what he called 'the world of work'.

Robert Woolf didn't mind, either, when I told him what the Metalwork teacher had said. He shrugged. He pointed out that most kids in our school probably will, in fact, end up working on the industrial estate, operating machines in the factories.

We were walking home from the Comp together. Through the old part of town. I was blushing. But, me? I was thinking. *I'm* not going to be in a factory. How could they think that?

It was as if Robert could read my mind. 'Why do you have to be any different? Why do you think you're so special?' He was red, too. He was furious with me, all of a sudden. And he was shouting so that others could hear.

I didn't say anything. Robert fitted in OK because he was a good footballer. That was all it took to make him fit in with the others. I didn't fit in with anyone. I felt like I was being cast off. It was no surprise to me that he simply ran away from me then. He was bored with the conversation, with me going on about having to do things like metalwork. He knew I was complaining really, just because I was scared of the machines. Before he ran off and left me behind that home-time, he said, 'You've gotta do things you don't want to do. You think you can just do the things you want and you're good at, that's your problem.'

I stared at him. What was he on about? And what about being bohemian? What about all the things he said when his sister was around? How come he was so keen to fit in at school? But then he was gone. He hared off down Burn Lane ahead of me.

But I was used to his betrayal by then. By that I don't mean the fact he'd been put in a different class to me, and his class seemed to have nicer people in it. He couldn't help which class he had been put into. By his betrayal I mean the first morning of the Comp, when he failed to come knocking at our door and made me late for my very first day.

It's dead embarrassing to think of now. I didn't even know the right way to walk to the Comp. I didn't want to walk across the claggy school fields on my first morning, even though that was the obvious way. I had to walk the long way, through the old housing estate, all around the edges, figuring the route out by myself.

I had waited in our kitchen with Mam till ten to nine. In my new tie and all my ironed stuff, name tags scratching at my skin. We had planned that Robert would come knocking for me at half past and we would walk down to school together. Bravely into

68

our future. Mam was glad I was going to have company. She was worried for me – having, perhaps, an idea about what my new place was going to be like. We had planned the morning like a military thing. I had been in my new clothes since seven-thirty. And we waited for Robert to turn up. Sure he must have been delayed. Surely he wouldn't have gone without me. At quarter to, Mam was phoning his house, but there was no answer. As I stood watching her listening to the ring at the other end in Brackett Close, I knew that Robert and his sister had already left for the Comp. His mam was out at work and their house was empty. And I was going to be late.

Then it was all fuss and flurry and flying out of the door. Just minutes ago we had been taking our time. Being almost ceremonial about it. Mam had taken a picture of me outside our front door. Me with my new school sports bag. Now I had to run like the clappers out of our estate, down Burn Lane, and through the nineteen-fifties streets. Skidding on dead leaves and mulch, heart pounding fit to burst. I'd be late and they would think I was a bad kid, a lazy kid. I'd start off on the wrong foot.

I went in through the main gates, about ten minutes late. The school was settling down for the morning. The low blocky buildings, all grey and olive green, were murmuring with a thousand bodies.

Tuesday

But everyone says that change is good.

Our new house is better than our old house. Mam says Brian will do his best to look after us, and be a new dad to me. Jacqui has moved in and that's great, isn't it? Having a new Nanna who lives with us, who likes some of the same things I do. Things are going to get better and better. This year I turn into a teenager, and that will be the biggest change yet. Mam says all of life will be different then. It is for everyone when you get to that age. You look at life through different eyes. I'm not sure I like the sound of that. But I think she's probably right. Everyone around me at school is changing and growing up. That's what they think.

The change I am thinking about today – this Tuesday early in the new year – is about the change in Doctors. And the start of the new season this evening. I'm thinking about the old Doctor, his body lying broken on the ground after his fatal fall from the top of a radio telescope. Having saved the universe again, at the end of last season, the Doctor sacrificed himself. We watched his life flash before his eyes, in the shape of all his old friends and enemies, and then his form started to shift and blur . . . It started to change . . . And all of a sudden he became the new Doctor. Young, unlined, bemused. Sitting up to confront his new life.

Now Robert and I are waiting for his first episode. Robert's got special permission from his mam to watch the start of the new season around our house. We spend the afternoon trying to fill in the time, listening to records and flipping through back issues of *Doctor Who Monthly*.

This change of Doctors might not be a change for the better at all. We don't know yet. But we sit all day Tuesday waiting. Things are moving on. Like they have to, apparently.

In the hour before The Show comes on, we finish our tea quickly. Then we're experimenting with sound levels in my bedroom.

Mam made us a special tea, one of my favourites. She made it in honour of my having a guest around, and also because it's a special day for us. We had potatoes baked in the oven till they're almost black on the outside. Opened and scooped out and mashed with red cheese, and then put back and toasted and loads of baked beans poured on top. It was like she wanted to make us our favourite thing for the night of The Show.

I was hoping that she and Brian wouldn't talk through The Show. The last time it was on – when they repeated some black-and-white classic episodes last summer – the two of them talked and it was hard not to tell them to shut up.

Upstairs Robert and I get the tape ready. I've got the Geoff Love version of the theme playing on my record player and Robert is pretending to be cool about it all. Being round at mine means he can't make his own cassette recording of The Show tonight, but he shrugs like that hardly matters.

'Seeing it once is enough. I used to tape it and listen again and again last year and stuff, and the year before. But now I reckon just watching once is enough.' Yeah, I think, but he'll probably be wanting to borrow my tapes pretty soon.

As we're making preparations and talking about the New Doctor and everything, there's a knock on my door and Jacqui's popping her head in. 'Hey guys,' she says, sounding impossibly exotic and American (I look to check that Robert is still impressed by my foreign new Nanna. He is, a bit! You can tell because he doesn't say a word, the whole time she's standing there.) 'I got you these, specially for watching your show tonight.' She holds out a crumpled paper bag of sweets. Jelly Babies! 'That's what he eats, isn't it? Your Doctor?'

I nod at her and she smiles, almost shyly back at us. I hand round the sugary babies and ask her if she'll be watching with us.

'Uh, I guess so,' she says. 'I'm pretty eager to, after the way you talk about it.'

Now the stakes are even higher. I hope it's good tonight. If it's not, I'll feel like I'm letting Jacqui down, as well as feeling mortified in front of Robert. Why can't I just watch The Show by myself? And check that it's okay before I watch it with others – and have all the pleasure to myself first?

Jacqui goes and Robert says to me, 'She's not, like, your real Nanna or anything, is she?'

The tape recordings are dead important to me – even if they're not to Robert Woolf.

Last November I got a tape recorder for my birthday, and it's one of my favourite things. Just a small, hand-held, battery-operated one. I've decided that I'm going to set it against the portable TV in my room and record the soundtracks of the new episodes of The Show. Robert did it with some episodes last year and the year before and he said it worked brilliantly. But he never kept the tapes! He used them to record himself, learning to play guitar.

Which seems like a waste to me. Why didn't he buy new tapes?

We experiment to see how loud the sound has to be. The local news comes booming out of the portable, and onto the landing. We play snippets back on the tape. It has to be pretty loud.

I've even made cassette covers for the first few episodes. I've copied drawings from publicity stills in the *Radio Times*.

'They're good,' Mam said, when I showed her. 'But . . . what if you don't like the new episodes? What if you want to rub over the recordings afterwards?'

I looked at her. *Don't like* the new episodes? *Rub over* them?

To make tape recordings permanent you have to pop the little plastic things out of the corners of the cassettes. That's what I'll be doing with my tapes from The Show. I'll have a whole collection for the new season.

We have to wait till the last minute and start recording upstairs just as the announcer comes on, saying what's coming on next. Then we have to back away, making sure that the tiny spools are going round and everything is working. The telly is booming as we tiptoe backwards out of the room.

*

Then Robert and I dash down the stairs, me first, to the living room, where the same thing is playing on the big telly. Brian is sitting there, eating peaches drowned in Carnation milk. He looks up at us dashing in. Mam follows us down the hall, bringing a tray with mugs of tea. Jacqui is already in place, looking politely expectant.

There's a pre-credits sequence! It's going as we run into the room. We're missing it! We're not settled yet! I don't even have to look at Robert to know that he's as cross as I am at missing precious seconds of The Show. They are starting the new season with a pre-credits teaser. They are showing the regeneration again. There's the old Doctor, lying almost dead in the grass, and surrounded by his young companions. Here's the moment he says goodbye and starts to glow with that unearthly light . . .

'I don't know,' Mam says, setting down the tray. 'Telly blaring upstairs, all down the landing. The same thing on down here. It's ridiculous! It's playing upstairs with no one watching it! What a waste of electricity!'

'Ma-aa-aam!' I protest. Then I stop because I realise I'm sounding whiney, which I don't want to do in front of Robert. The two of us are sitting on the floor between the telly and the settee. The adults are on the settee behind us, talking too much. Jacqui is in her place by her coffee table, watching with interest. I glance back now and then to see her frowning over her glasses in concentration.

'Why can't you watch it upstairs?' Mam asks, right over the title sequence and music starting. I get that familiar gut-churning when I hear the music. And there's the new Doctor's face in the title sequence, forming out of the stars.

I've already explained to Mam what we're hoping to do. Taping the soundtracks and making a collection. 'It's on upstairs for the tape, Mam,' I tell her, turning round briefly.

'Oh, yeah,' she says. 'But what's the good if you don't see the pictures? You won't be able to tell what's going on . . .'

Which is sort of true in a way, but isn't.

We drink the new episode in. We absorb every detail, and not even Mam and Brian chuntering on behind us can distract us now. We are storing up all the visuals and the story details and twists and turns and the expressions on the faces of our favourite characters . . . and we will play them back in our heads as we listen to the soundtrack again in the dark.

And the episode . . . ?

It's amazing! The Doctor's got post-regeneration

trauma. So he's wandering about inside the laby-rinthine corridors of the TARDIS, unravelling his old scarf and not quite sure who he's meant to be. It seems so weird, seeing this different man in the old Doctor's things. I love it when the Doctor's mind drifts and he starts to think he's his previous selves. He does impersonations of the earlier Doctors and refers to K9, Jamie and Vicki. I love all that stuff. Both Robert and I have read all the novelisations we could get our hands on, so we know all the people from the past he mentions. I wonder whether Jacqui has understood it all. It was maybe a bit complicated for someone new to it all.

'That was pretty good,' she nods. 'Maybe I didn't quite get *all* of it . . . I'm not an expert like you guys.'

And the Master is back! He had to be, after the end of the last season. In his black velvet outfit, abducting the Doctor's companion Adric, and string-ing him up in a huge spider's web. Plotting further schemes to finish off the Time Lord. While the Doctor is at his most vulnerable, and recovering from the shock of changing his form, the Master sends the TARDIS spinning back through time to the beginning of the universe and the biggest explo-sion there's ever been . . .

'I didn't know what was going on,' Mam says. 'It's not very real, is it?'

That's the end of the episode! The cliffhanger, with noxious hot steam starting to fill the interior of the console room. The music comes bursting on and Mam calls out: 'So that's the end of that! You'll have to wait to find out what happens now!'

It takes a moment to disengage from the screen and the story. Mam's getting Brian to pass her the remote. 'Quick! *Coronation Street* is on!'

Robert and I are still thinking about the hydrogen in-rush, the Doctor's new cricketing outfit and his disordered mind – and the way he mentioned Ice Warriors! Wouldn't it be great if they came back? And we turn and run out of the room as swiftly as we came in. We want to check the tape came out OK. We want to run it back and listen again straight away.

'You keep that sound down!' Mam yells after us. 'You'll have them neighbours going mental at us!'

And now she's turned to ITV, there are two channels playing full blast in our house. As we run up the stairs it's suddenly really noisy round ours.

Wednesday

Wednesday is the day that we are officially declared snowed in.

That's not to say that we can't move around, or even get out of our houses. We can still do as much as we ever did, only a bit slower, as the snow has frozen in translucent layers across the roads and pavements. It makes going down town, over the Burn and down Burn Lane, rather tricky. Wednesday morning, I make the trip to the precinct with Mam and at one point we have to hold hands, inching our way over the ice.

We visit the small town library, taking back the *Doctor Who* books I had over Christmas, swapping them for new ones. We queue in the rent office, and the post office and the bank, and all the talk we can hear is about the snow. How nothing can get in or out of our town. We are sealed off from the world.

I keep going over and over last night's episode in my mind. How it doesn't seem there are going to be any monsters in this story. On one hand, I think that's a shame. But then, maybe I prefer the more realistic stories, with actual people in them. I'm wondering how soon the novelisation will be in the shops.

We're queueing in the stuffy, over-warm electricity shop when Mam gets a panic attack.

'I can't wait any more, let's get out,' she cries, getting all flustered. She jams her papers and the cash back in her bag and she's whirling around and pushing past the others in the queue. 'I need to get out,' she says, and I follow her back to the precinct.

Sometimes shopping days are just queueing up like this. Making payments at the different offices, picking up cash at the post office. When I come down to do the shopping by myself, Mam entrusts me with all the different envelopes and different forms and official papers. It's complicated but rewarding, doing all the messages.

Today they're only half done, but Mam has had enough. We turn back, fetching pasties from the cake shop, just as the sky darkens and readies for snow.

Later that afternoon, Robert Woolf calls round again. He's all wrapped up in his football scarf and his new parka. He's brought Karen's exercise book for me to have a look at. So I can read her novel. 'I've finished it. I thought it might give you some ideas.'

I'm not sure what Karen would think about him passing around her private things. I give him back his *Auton Invasion* and his *Day of the Daleks*. When I start talking again about last night's episode, he gives a noncommittal shrug. 'Not much happened really, did it?' he says.

I stare at him. Last night he was as excited about it as I was. He loved all that post-regenerative trauma and those touches of continuity. And he especially said how he liked them exploring the interior dimensions of the TARDIS.

But now he just squinches up his face and says, 'Anyway, you know, I think I might be, like, going off it.'

I can't believe this! 'Going off it?'

He shrugs. 'I'll give it another episode or two. But that's it. I thought about it a bit last night and, really, I don't like the new Doctor much, do you?'

I listened to the recording of the episode on my tape player twice more before falling asleep last night. But I don't say this. Because I don't *like* the new Doctor, I *love* him! The thought of that startles me. Thank god I never said 'love' in front of Robert.

The polite thing would be to ask Robert in. It's snowing heavily now and he's standing at our side door with flakes settling on him.

But I don't think today's a good day to have

company round. Mam's lying down this afternoon. Her panic is turning into a migraine. She says she's got the flashing lights, all turning in circles inside her head. I imagine her migraines are just like the title sequence of The Show. Swirling and scintillating like the start of an episode. She's lying down and she wouldn't want kids running about in the house.

'I'm off down the Burn to have a muck about,' Robert tells me. 'Are you coming? We can crack the ice in the Burn and lob some snowballs and stuff.'

I'd better not. It'd be bad to leave Mam alone in the house for the afternoon if she's feeling unwell.

Jacqui's out all day too, so she's no help. She's joined a club for Senior Citizens at the Rec, though she isn't keen on being around a bunch of old folk, she says. Still, she went off this morning for their coffee hour, a gentle exercise class and a swim. Then a late lunch. I can't imagine her being forced to socialise all day. Surely she'd rather slope off and read by herself? After her new club she's off to the library for the rest of the afternoon. I think she feels she has to be out of Mam's hair, some days.

I snap back into the present moment with Robert, and start to make my excuses about not going out, when I hear familiar voices coming up the empty street.

'Well?' Robert asks me again.

'I can't,' I tell him. I'm glad I've got an excuse now. 'Here's my Big Nanna turning up. Surprise visit.'

Robert scowls, turning to look at the two old women shuffling through the snow. 'I'm off,' he tells me, shoving his *Doctor Who* books into his parka pockets. I stow Karen's exercise book in my jeans back pocket.

Here comes my Big Nanna with her best friend, Daisy. They are all wrapped up against the cold. They are covered in fresh-fallen snow, all red-faced and laughing with the exertion. They hurry up to us and when my Nanna pats my cheek her hand is frozen red. 'We made it! Let us in!'

Her friend Daisy does her huge laugh at me, and hurries into our front hall with my Nanna.

But how? How did they get here? Our town is meant to be sealed off. We've been snowed in!

'Ee, I'm bursting for the loo,' my Nanna says. 'And so is Daisy. We've walked all over them, whatcha-callits, fields and what have you. All the way from the main road. Our bus couldn't get through the snow.'

'You've walked over fields?' I ask them, taking their coats. 'How did you manage that?'

'Pshaw, nothing to it,' my Nanna says, heading for the stairs. 'Not for two tough old birds like we are!

Now, I'd better get myself to the toilet. Where's your Mam?'

'She's lying down . . .'

My Nanna starts heading up the stairs, calling out in a loud voice. 'Lying down, is she? Ee, in the middle of the afternoon, our Mary! That's no good! Stop hiding behind your pillow . . . !'

I just know that, lying down in her room, my Mam's heart will be sinking. It'll be like an anchor drifting surely to the ocean bed. She'll think she's dreaming. Then she'll realise, no: Irene is here. Her mother is visiting.

She always visits without warning. 'As if she's trying to catch me out,' Mam grumbles. 'As if she thinks I'm up to something. But what could I be up to? What's she hoping to see?'

My Big Nanna wears a camel-hair coat and she clutches a brown shiny handbag under her bosom and goes about like the Queen on walkabout. She examines everything round our house like Her Majesty visiting a factory in a foreign land. That's the sucky-lemon-faced look she wears.

Her friend Daisy is deaf and always in tow. Daisy is always more effusive and excitable than my Nanna. She has no family of her own, we've been told. No kids, no grandchildren, and so she flings herself into other people's family gatherings whole-heartedly.

My nanna always says, 'She's not self-conscious in the slightest. Especially when her hearing aids aren't working. Daisy can show her feelings more than the rest of us.'

Soon we are sitting at the pine table in the kitchen. My nanna is looking around, seeing if she can spot something newly bought. Something to examine or admire. 'Ee, our Mary,' she will say. 'This is all new, these place mats and cups and saucers and what-have-you. You spend too much! It's all spend-spend-spend round here! You'll never have anything saved up. It's always like a shop when you come round here. Everything brand bally new!'

'What?' Daisy squinches up her face to hear.

Mam is washing cups at the sink. She's wincing. She looks likes she's still got a migraine.

'I said, Daisy, that our Mary's always buying new bally stuff! Spending her money! Money what she hasn't got, prob'ly!'

'Uh-hoh, uh-hoh,' Daisy agrees. She looks at Mam and grins. 'Ee, it's lovely, pet. Lovely to see you and David.'

'How's Brian? And how's his mother settling in? Big move, moving into someone else's home. Doing all right, is she?' Without waiting for an answer, Big Nanna pops her sheepskin gloves into her shopping bag and stares down into her milkless tea. 'I hope

86

this is weak enough for me. And don't make me drink more than two cups. Last time I was wanting the toilet all the way back home.' She lives a two-hour bus ride away, all the way to Tyneside. In the snow it'll be even longer.

We watch Nanna test her tea. 'Bassy-go-go!' she cries, quickly blowing on it. 'That's hot! That's scalding hot, our Mary!'

Mam rolls her eyes. I always like it when my Big Nanna comes out with one of her explosive shouts of, 'Sally-ha-ha!' or 'Bassy-go-go!' I haven't got a clue what she's on about, or where those phrases come from. They sound like a different language to me. Mam says she's having a throwback moment. Back to her descendants in the distant past. When Mam says this, I stare at my nanna. I am fascinated by the idea that she might really be something out of history.

'Your nanna comes from deepest, darkest Norfolk,' Mam has told me, more than once. 'She came up from there during the war.'

And I find myself staring at my Big Nanna like she is a creature from another world.

'I expect that Brian's mam is missing her independence, though, living here with you lot,' Big Nanna says. 'I wouldn't like to lose my independence. My own place. Neither would you, eh, Daisy?'

Today Mam is distracted by the rinse Nanna has put into her hair, especially for the festive season. Usually she opts to turn her perm a mahogany colour, but this time it has a distinctly reddish tinge. 'You've dyed your hair ginger,' Mam cries, and I can see she's holding back from laughing. I keep quiet. Usually it's best to, during visits like this. It's much more fun just watching the adults from the sidelines.

Mam's right, though. In the clear light of the kitchen, Nanna's hair looks a funny colour.

'Ginger, by hang!' Big Nanna shouts out. Her thick eyebrows arch up and her cheeks flush. 'You cheeky little thing! Ginger!'

Daisy continues to nod and smile. 'Oh-huh,' she says. 'Ee, aye.'

'It's a bit red,' Mam says. 'Russet.'

Nanna's face is burning now. Her hair-dye experiments are a sore spot. Last time her perm thinned at the crown, where she'd been slapping the solution on. 'She's calling me a ginger, Daisy! She's saying I've made myself a gingernut!'

Daisy blinks and laughs. 'Eee!'

'The cheeky beggar,' Nanna goes on. 'What does she know? She dyes her bally hair as well. She should know Deep Mahogany when she sees it.' Then she seizes up her bag and takes out some parcels. 'Anyway,

I've brung up some little cakes for you. And some sausage rolls, only party bite-sized, mind. Don't give me nothing, I can't eat, with my stomach.' She sips her tea. 'That's a bit less scalding now.'

We watch as she swirls her dark tea in the cup, and then sucks her molten sugar off her spoon. 'And what's better than one cup of tea?' she asks me in her ritual way, suddenly brightening.

'Two cups of tea!' I chime.

Mam is setting out cakes and sausage rolls on plates. She doesn't say this is our second lot of stuff from the cake shop today.

'Here, look at these!' Nanna says proudly. She has slipped her shoes off and is holding them up so we can see. They are her usual court shoes, but now they've got metal tread things on the bottom. They are like man traps, hinged and spiky. 'Snow-treads!' she announces. 'I sent off a coupon in the *Daily Mirror*. They keep a lovely grip in the snow.'

'Uh-hoh,' Daisy says. 'They're smashing, aren't they?'

'Did you send off for some as well, Daisy?' Mam shouts.

'Uh-hoh, I did. Aye.'

Big Nanna rolls her eyes. 'No, she didn't. She's just saying that to chime in. You couldn't trust her with something sharp like these. Mind, she's always falling over. Aren't you, Daisy hinny? You're always falling over?'

Daisy seems to cotton on. 'Oh, aye.'

'She's a danger to herself. She goes round laughing all the time and not watching where she's going,' Nanna says. 'Aren't you?'

'Aye, aye, I am.'

'I wish I was a bit more like her,' Mam says. 'Laughing at everything like that.'

Nanna pulls a face.

Time to retire to the front room for a bit, to sit on the settee with their knitting and a further cup of tea.

'You've got all your decorations down, I see,' Nanna says approvingly. 'I took ours down on Boxing Day.' This is a dig, for our not going to see her during Christmas. Her tree each year is the same: a threadbare silver affair on a green stand, with tinsel so ratty and sharp it could cut you to ribbons. All the ornaments are glass shells, sprayed silver. Something about that tree always makes me feel sad.

I watch Nanna and Daisy take out their knitting, once they are comfortable on the settee. Mam perches herself on the armchair and tugs her Readicut rug box towards her. As the clicking from the ladies' needles begins in earnest – a busy, consoling sound – Mam looks almost shy about pulling out her canvas tapestry, and showing off her half-done tiger.

'You've got this room lovely,' Daisy says. 'Lovely, pet.'

Mam smiles and hefts up her tiger tapestry. This is the most recent of a whole load of woollen tapestry rugs she has made in recent years. They arrive in boxes through the post and you get a large canvas mat, cartons of coloured wool cut to the exact right length and two special tagging tools with pincers at the end. She used to make those rugs before, in the old house. She made a few winter scenes, with stark, black trees against a red winter sun and all this whiteness. They were really effective. They were wall-hangings, not like rugs that people walk on and mucky up. Right now she is doing a challenging one, in loads of different colours.

'Eee!' Daisy cries. 'Look at that!'

Nanna takes her glasses out of her case. She puts them on and peers over the top. She purses her mouth. 'What the devil's that meant to be, then?'

'It's a tiger!' Daisy bellows.

'I wish I'd never ordered it now and just stuck with the winter pictures,' Mam says. 'It's too complicated.'

It is a Bengal tiger darting out of the forest and coming straight at you. The whole rug is as tall as she is. Nanna is staring the beast straight in the eye. She looks down at the bobble hat she is on with. 'Aye, well. They're always finding some way to part you from your money.' She glares at Mam.

They fall quiet. Mam looks down at her tapestry rug, sighs, and starts fiddling with the special tagging tool. She's very skilled with it, tagging on the threads of wool. The pincers go clicking all night as we watch TV, usually. They pause occasionally as she selects the right colour from the cartons of wool. As usual I am dying to have a go and help out. I know she has a spare tagging tool. But she never wants any help. It would spoil the look of the tapestry, she says. 'You have to do all the holes in the right sequence,' she says. 'They have to come out at exactly the right length. Otherwise the rug will look scraggy and unprofessional.'

She knows I want to have a go because she is as far down as the Bengal tiger's blazing eyes. That looks like the most exciting bit. The burning orange and smoky amber of its eyes.

'What's this you were saying on the phone?' Nanna asks Mam suddenly. 'What's all this about that Jacqui sleepwalking? And going about the streets in the night? What does she think she's doing? And where is she today, anyway, by the way?'

Mam says, 'Oh, she's got her new Seniors Club

today at the Rec . . . And then she spends hours in the library. And there's a café she hangs out in, with some of the old people in the precinct . . .'

'Oh, she does, does she?' says Big Nanna, pursing her lips. 'Keeping herself busy, then. Since she's been widowed.' Big Nanna clearly disapproves of Jacqui. I don't know why. They never really got on the few times they've met.

Mam says, 'The other night, she just about gave us all a nervous breakdown. We were hunting the streets. Got the neighbours out of their beds! She could have wandered out onto the main road! She could be dead or anything.'

Daisy's smiling, and I can tell she hasn't heard half of what Mam has said. Mam could well be explaining the plot of some soap opera she'd been watching.

'Have you heard this, Daisy?' Nanna shouts out. 'About the silly woman walking about the streets in her nightie?'

'Oh, uh-hoh,' says Daisy, and it's not clear whether she's heard or not.

'Aye, well,' Nanna says. 'You have to make sure you're all locked up at night. You can't have her wandering the streets, our Mary. Not in this bally day and age. Ee, I don't know. She could have been dead of pneumonia or anything. A bad man could have grabbed her.'

93

Mam's gritting her teeth. She's wishing she never told Big Nanna now. Now it looks like it's all Mam's fault. 'She managed to unlock the door in her sleep and everything. She was away! There was nothing we could have done.'

Big Nanna tells her, 'You'll have the burglars in. Killing you in your beds. Won't she, Daisy?'

'Ee, aye, she will.'

'This is a bally rough estate you live on, our Mary,' Big Nanna says. 'Mind, everywhere's rough these days. Our estate's getting rough, an' all, isn't it, Daisy?'

'Jacqui's still in mourning . . .' says Mam. 'It's only recently, after all, since her Arnold died. She's still in shock, poor thing . . .'

It sounds weird to me, to hear Mam defending Jacqui like this, and imagining what her feelings might be. My Big Nanna's looking sceptical. She thinks Jacqui's fond of drawing attention to herself. She has never said as much, outright. But somehow she implies it, with little things she says, and expressions she pulls, whenever Jacqui is the topic of conversation.

Big Nanna looks like she's miles away for a second. Then she says, 'You know, I went sleep-walking for a while. I'd forgotten all about it, till just then. But I did, you know. And I got my way outside. It was when we were living with my mother-in-law.

94

When I first went to South Shields. This were during the war. Well, it were a new place. I was all . . . disorientated, whatever the word is. But I was getting up in the night. I was walking about all over. They followed me one night. They say I went as far as the Marine Park! Right near the beach! They say I could have been walking into the water. But they were too scared to wake me up . . .'

We're all staring at Big Nanna. She smiles, and goes back to her knitting. Her voice has turned gentle, quite different. She's saying things as she pictures them and remembers them, inside her head.

'But I settled down eventually and I stopped. It's just something that happens. New places, new things. It's the mind's way of coping with new circumstances, whatever you call them. I don't know. But it happens sometimes. It's a way of reacting to things that are new.'

I realise that I'm staring at Big Nanna. She smiles at me, and I grin back. Her hair looks more maroon than ginger, I think.

Then Big Nanna starts telling Mam about being in the bingo recently in South Shields, and bumping unexpectedly into my dad's parents. Being cold-shouldered by my Little Nanna and my Granda. They were dressed up to the nines, studiously ignoring her. The old man made a great show of pulling up a chair for my Little Nanna and treating her like a lady. 'Silly old fool,' Big Nanna says. 'He's like her slave. They go rubbing everyone's nose in it. How they're supposed to be so well-off and happy and known by everyone. Waving to people like they're famous. And she still dresses like she's forty years younger.'

I feel sick every time Big Nanna mentions seeing my other grandparents in her town. I haven't seen them in two years, not since Dad died. That side of our family, as Mam says, seem to be a finished chapter in our lives. They don't want anything more to do with us now. Maybe they don't like the idea of Brian moving in. Of Mam having a new life now.

Mam and my Big Nanna go on trading stories, repeating dialogue, doing the voices, imitating every quirk and gesture of the people they tell tales on. They always do this. I sit listening, agog, and Daisy knits – pitching in with random, 'Uh-hoh's.'

Mam and Big Nanna talk up a storm, until it's time for the old ladies to go off, back across the snow, to the edge of the town, and catch a bus.

Mam always says things like, 'I don't know. I just can't talk to my own Mam. Why is that?'

But she does. They talk loads. They always do.

One of my presents for Christmas was a Polaroid camera. This is just the kind of occasion it was meant for. I bring it down, with flashbulbs and film, before they leave. We all crouch on the living-room floor. Daisy makes us squash together and grin. She barks out laughing and checks that everyone else is doing the same.

Big Nanna says, 'She's always laughing. She doesn't have a care in the world, does she?'

The rest of us are always so self-conscious in front of cameras. I frame them in the view-finder.

'I say, Daisy, you don't have a care, do you?' Big Nanna laughs.

'Smile!' Daisy shouts. 'Everyone smile for the bally picture!'

We do, and we take turns snapping each other in different combinations. We hold up the small, square prints and watch as they develop. The blues, yellows, greens and reds rise slowly out of the flat grey. The instant camera clicks, whirrs and flashes, again and again.

'Smile!'

SPRING TERM,
MARCH

Monday

Lately I've made a friend who's a girl. Not a girl-friend – that's not what I mean.

At breaktime and lunchtime we walk around the perimeter of the school buildings. We loop the loop and talk like mad all the way. Round the PE block, through the middle bit with the language lab, round all four house blocks, and down the side of the school hall. We walk round about ten times each day, hardly noticing the drab scenery we pass by, or the hordes of kids. We're usually immersed in our conversation and we walk along as if in a trance, listening intently to each other.

Of course, people shout stuff out as we pass by. Derogatory stuff and things you'd rather not hear. Rude stuff, sometimes. It's worse round the back of the sports hall, overlooking the rank, tangled mass of the Burn. Here, hard kids are always smoking, out of range of the teachers, and they scowl at us as we pass by. But it is like we are protected somehow, inside the bubble of our friendship and our private talk.

Karen Doyle is the cleverest person I've ever met.

She's good at everything at school. She gets the best marks in her class for all their subjects and she wears it very lightly. 'The thing is,' she tells me, 'the way they do things here, it's just learning things like a parrot. So if you've got a good memory, you've got it made. There's nothing clever about that. It's just reciting back to them what they want to hear.'

Karen's got a brilliant memory – photographic – so she does really well. I look at her and imagine hundreds of thousands of pictures and pages and tables and graphs and diagrams all rolled up and tucked away safely inside her head. I would love to have the same but, when I need to learn something, I have to sit for hours on end, repeating it, copying it out, chanting it.

'It doesn't encourage original thought,' Karen says, with a shrug. 'But that's not what they really want, is it?' She turns to me and grins as we walk along past the netball court's jangling wire fence. Her eyes are this very intense, sparkling blue. Her hair is purple this week, frizzed and crimped in a New Romantic style. She's wearing a long black cardigan-shawl thing and owlish glasses. She and her friends in Class 1M have this whole grannyish look going on. The clever girls do, at any rate. They wear black fishnet stockings and pencil-narrow skirts and creamy-coloured blouses with lacy bits.

Even though I'm in my normal uniform, just like everyone else, and even though I'm a lad and everything, Karen still wants to talk to me and tell me her ideas about having original thoughts, and how we're not supposed to be having them. She doesn't make me feel hopeless, like Robert Woolf sometimes does. Robert tells me that he and his sister are different, alternative, esoteric. He explains to me how they aren't conventional or mainstream and he tells me how important it is to find your own style. Find your own thing. Your bag. But at the same time he makes it seem impossible for me.

'How can you find your own style,' he says, 'when you never go out? You're always staying indoors. You never do anything. You think about that Show of yours and that's about it. You aren't . . .' He was seething. He's been losing patience with me recently. 'You aren't expanding your horizons.' The funny thing was, as he was lambasting me like this, in his dark kitchen one morning, he was using one of those squashy, slidey chest-expander machines. He was huffing and puffing as he manipulated the daft-looking thing, and telling me I should expand my outlook on the world. And it made me feel tired. It made me feel that being as individual as Robert and his sister was work as hard as Robert's exercise regime. And that looked hard enough. Every time I talked to him he was flexing or squatting or doing what he called 'reps'.

Karen isn't like that. She makes me feel that I am already alternative and different and a complete individual. I am doing all the right things already, and I don't have to struggle to be anyone else. To be more interesting than I already am. I don't know why she feels this way, or has this confidence in who she thinks I am. But I like it. When we walk round and round the school each weekday I feel like I can say anything I want to her. I can bring anything up as the next topic of conversation. And she won't be bored or think it's silly. She'll listen with that serious expression, head cocked slightly towards me, eyes sparkling with her own thoughts.

Like Robert's sister, she wears some kind of hippy-ish perfume. Once, briefly, she was Robert's first girlfriend, back in the autumn term for a week or two, so perhaps she got her perfume from the same shop as Robert's sister. She gave me a packet of incense sticks she bought in Darlington. I was to light them as I listened to the compilation tape she had made me, of all her favourite songs. When I asked at home for some matches though, Mam was immediately suspicious. 'Don't you start on them fags. My dad was ill because of them. So was Brian's dad. Dead before they should have been. Don't you start!'

I'd no intention. I wanted to light my jossticks

and listen to T-Rex, Ian Dury, Siouxsie and the Banshees. I borrowed some headphones, listening to Karen's tape on my little machine in the night.

Also, unbeknownst to her, I read her ongoing novel by torchlight. Shocked and avidly turning pages, being as quiet as possible.

Robert has told me that her fellow writers have dropped out of the novel-writing project. There has been some in-fighting, about the way the endless, sexy story was going. The other girls were wanting more realism. They think it has become too far-fetched. Karen doesn't care about that. 'It's a fantasy, isn't it? I want it to be fantastic.' And now she writes her novel by herself, late at night, devoting to it the time she saves on schoolwork with her photographic memory. And she lends Robert the current volume of her opus, which he secretly passes onto me and I smuggle into our house to read at night. God knows what would happen if Mam found it amongst my stuff, so I keep it at the bottom of my school bag for safe-keeping.

Karen's novel is becoming wilder, weirder, and much, much ruder, with every passing day. She never mentions it to me, but she's interested in hearing about the things that I write.

'So,' she says to me. 'When do I get to read something of yours?'

This is as we walk anticlockwise on a spring-like

day in March. The bright air is swirling around us and everything smells fresh and new. I'm not imagining it. Today it feels like the seasons have switched over. I haven't even brought a coat with me today. I'm walking around in my baggy green jumper, even though Mam said I was over-optimistic as I left the house. But I feel like being over-optimistic. Mam can't believe the way I'm just about skipping out of the house on my way to the comp. Me, who went dragging my heels and hating it all through the winter. This is how I feel now I've got a new friend. That's all it takes, it seems.

But Karen's looking at me too searchingly. I try to fob her off. 'Oh, I don't know. Nothing's finished. Nothing's good enough. I just . . .' She knows I have been writing properly since the start of the new year. Back when the Christmas holidays finished and we got extra days at home when the town was snowed in. Frozen pipes ruptured and burst all over the Comp, and the water froze again and school was impossible for a further two, delirious, wonderful, snowy weeks. And I started to write. Spurred on by the example of Karen and her notebooks – even though I didn't know her well at all at that point (and now it seems like a different era entirely) – I bought some exercise books and plunged into a story of my own.

But I haven't shown it to anyone yet.

Tuesday

Here I am in the middle of the night with my hand-writing getting scrawlier and smaller, writing for hours on end on the thick-lined pages of exercise books I bought in WHSmiths. Like I said to Karen, there's nothing written yet that I'm ready for anyone else to read. I'm not even sure what it is I'm writing yet. I'm just getting some writing done.

I'm stringing out sentence after sentence and it's like flinging a lasso rope about my head. Aiming wildly for what it is I want to say, and throwing the line as hard as I can: hoping it will tie something down. Chains of words go marching out across the rough pages of my books. Some pages have only a couple of words on. Some are completely chock-a-block, bright blue with scribbled words. Others are crossed out and obliterated by wild, scratchy lines. Stories are started, toyed with, tinkered with and abandoned. Other stories begin in their stead. I have ideas, burn them out, use them up, and try out new ones.

I have messed about with this stuff for weeks now,

as the dregs of winter faded and the world warmed up. The black brick and tarmac of our estate warmed through and the Burn blossomed for a while, pink, yellow and frothy white. By the time everything turned seething green and the New Season is almost finished, I've found I've written several slim books' worth of stuff. I don't pause to read anything back. Not yet. I don't want to be put off or disheartened. I don't want to find – just yet – that I have wasted my time writing page upon page of rubbish.

I try to write about normal stuff and real people. But, what happens? The characters from *Doctor Who*, or from Marvel comics keep creeping in. They turn up and get all involved in the action. At the moment I'm writing about London after a nuclear war and Spiderman has come over from America to team up with the Fourth Doctor and K9 to fight the Daleks in the post-nuclear wilderness, which is, of course, inhabited by hideous mutants that the Daleks have made their slaves. It's a pretty good story, especially the banter between Spiderman and the Doctor.

But what would people say if I told them what I was writing? They'd think it was stupid.

In another, Batman and the Joker work together to rid Gotham City of the monsters that are somehow taking over: Frankenstein's Monster, Dracula, and the Mummy. And then there's the one about the *Enterprise* from *Star Trek* orbiting the Planet of the Apes, and we see how Spock and Kirk react to General Urko and his gorilla soldiers.

Sometimes I get these ideas going and the story is rattling along, when another idea occurs to me, and I drop the original one. Stories break off halfway through, or right at their beginnings. If I read back through, everything seems tangled and chopped up. I can't seem to get anything finished. Not yet, anyway.

But there's a great sense of power. Whole worlds come into existence because I write a sentence or two about them. Whole characters appear. Things happen, because I will them to. It takes little energy, or even effort.

I sit under my desk. Leaning on my bed. The books are splayed open on my continental quilt. I write in pencil, and I love the pauses to sharpen them to a deadly point in the wickerwork bin: I love that woody scent and blunting them busily again as I plunge into the story. And I go into a kind of trance.

But everything I write is implausible. I know that. Everything I'm doing is ridiculous. Those dimensional portals between the waste ground that used to be London and the Planet of the Apes, are something I have conveniently arranged, so that Doctor Who and Spiderman can meet the crew of the *Enterprise*. Now there can be a great big battle between them and the apes and the nuclear mutants who have, of course, joined forces also.

Even when I'm downstairs having tea, I'm seeing the stories unwind in my head. I'm eating with my family, spooning up jam sponge and custard. I'm even talking with them, and taking part in their conversations, and making plans with them. But I'm really back in the midst of that story upstairs, which lies there waiting for me. My story waits with a me-sized doorway right in its middle. My story knows it isn't going anywhere without me.

Sometimes I watch telly with the others and it'll be some rubbish ITV sitcom that's on. Or some rotten quiz show, just the same as all the others. And I'll want to be back upstairs, making stuff up. I'll get up and slip upstairs without a word. I think they think I'm moody and huffy, going about scowling and frowning and keeping the words inside my head. I nip up to my room and sit there alone and Mam even starts to worry about it. Am I facing adolescence? Am I turning into a teenager? Are these patches of solitude and silence just part of the big changes coming my way?

I don't know either.

'You used to be a cheerful kid. Friendly and happy. You used to be a proper chatterbox. Why have you gone all quiet? What's happened to all your talk?' My mam bites her lip and frets like this. Maybe she blames herself.

I heft out the toy typewriter I've had since I was a kid. I forgot about it. It's a blue plastic model with white keys, and it's right at the back of the walk-in cupboard, behind racks of coats and old clothes and bin bags stuffed with things we're not using. This is an old toy, too young for me now. But it's a type-writer. And, when I try it out in my room, holding my breath, it seems to still work enough. The keys rattle happily and the skinny arms clatter about, printing letters that are only a little bit faded and smudgy.

On my next trip to the town precinct I buy a brown-paper parcel of typewriting paper. Fifty sheets of A5, which is the largest size that will go in my old typewriter. But it doesn't matter. I'm going to teach myself to do this properly. I'm going to turn the clutter and scrawl of my pencil marks into something real. I'm going to turn it into a proper story.

Tuesday night

Robert Woolf calls on me and he's got his heavy bag of free papers with him. This is his new job and he's been doing it the past three weeks: delivering the free advertising paper to every house and flat on our estate. It takes him about three hours each Tuesday night and he gets a penny for every paper he delivers. I've been walking round with him each week, straight after The Show has been on.

Tonight I burst out of the house. 'Did you see it?'

He frowns. He's wearing his new black bomber jacket that his gran bought him. I'm wearing a jumper and no coat: this is how much warmer the nights are now. 'See what?' he goes.

'The Show!'

'Oh, yeah,' he says. 'Course. It was OK, wasn't it?'

I shout ta-ra down our hall and slam the front door. 'OK? It was fantastic!' I follow him down our street and the air is soft. The sun has slipped below the blocky shapes of the flats. The most recent episodes of The Show have been about the Cybermen. Those evil silver giants coming back was enough of a surprise, but tonight something really shocking has happened in The Show. At the climax of the story, just when you thought the Doctor was about to rescue one of his companions – Adric – from certain death . . . the Doctor failed. Adric was killed. The space freighter he was aboard crashed into the Earth back in prehistoric times and killed all the dinosaurs. 'It was amazing! They really killed him off! They had silence at the end instead of the theme tune, and everything!'

Robert is loping along with his usual long stride, rolling up free papers to get them ready as he goes. 'Well, he was an annoying, whingey character, anyway. I hated him.'

'I know,' I say. 'But still, it was a bit of a shock. This Season has been brilliant, hasn't it? There's only four more episodes left. What's going to happen when it finishes? It'll be awful!'

Robert tuts. 'It's only a TV show.'

'Yeah, but . . . it's not, is it? It's The Show.'

He rolls his eyes at me. He starts on the terrace of black houses at the end of our cul-de-sac. He flings open the first gate, dashes up the path, thrusts the paper through the letterbox and beats a hasty retreat. He leaves the garden gate open behind him. He does each house in about two seconds flat. 'I don't know if anybody ever reads this paper,' he says. 'At home, we just chuck ours out.'

Mam does the competitions in ours. She won a huge cuddly Snoopy last Christmas. It was brought by a couple of newspaper men in a box, right before Christmas, and she was delighted. She had never won anything before in her life, she said. The men took a picture for the paper of her and me and Brian, sitting with Snoopy in our front room. Snoopy was wearing a tam o'shanter (a Scottish hat) and a little coat, for some reason. He now sits in front of our wood-effect fire, as if warming himself at the hearth. He has pride of place in our front room.

I watch Robert going up and down several paths, clashing gates and snapping letterboxes. A few gardens have grumbling and yapping dogs. They lurk about in yards studded with clods of dog poo. When it comes to these homes, Robert simply hurls a rolled-up paper in the general direction of the door.

We pass the play park with the giant metal snail thing, and into the next street, and the next one. The street lights are starting to glow an uncertain pink and yellow and the air is turning dim. Lights are coming on: the pebbly steamy warmth of bathroom windows, and the yolky glow of kitchens. Times like these, our estate seems a cosy place, with everyone squashed in so closely. I am suddenly aware of the presence of so many people, pressed in together. I breathe in the evening scents of the blossom on the spindly council trees, mixed with the papery, pulpy, inky smell of Robert's free papers.

'What's happening with you and Karen?' he asks me suddenly.

We come to one of the flat blocks, four storeys high. Its doorway seems forbiddingly dark. When we step inside, the smell is pretty awful. People must come in here to have a wee for a laugh, which must be horrible for the residents.

'Nothing's happening,' I tell him, and my voice sounds squeaky and hollow in the stairwell, as I follow him up. I hiss, 'We're not, like, boyfriend and girlfriend, or anything.'

'People think you are,' he says, looking back. 'Karen's a nice girl. Why aren't you an item? The way you go walking round with each other. Swapping notes all the time . . . People have noticed.'

I sigh. 'It's just not like that. We're friends. Can't I just have a friend who's a girl?'

Robert whistles. 'People are interested in what goes on. You should go out with her, I think. She's a good kisser.' We pause on the first landing, where the smell is even worse. I look out of the window at the view of the estate. The idea of kissing Karen seems strange. And the way Robert mentioned it, like that, made it seem that he's proud of his former connection with her. Like he's got first dibs. He's always showing off about something, I suddenly think. Like that heavy paper bag. The first time he came round wearing it he made a big show of making me lift it up and put it on, and I was amazed by the weight of all those papers. My legs buckled and he laughed, taking it back off me. Even his ability to carry a heavy bag is something to crow about. But these are awful thoughts to have about someone who's meant to be a best friend.

'We're friends,' I tell him. I reach for a phrase familiar from the soaps we watch at home. 'There isn't anything else between us.' And I'm quite pleased with the effect. I watch a purple and burnt orange dusk settle over the dark canyons of the black houses.

Robert leads the way up to the next storey. 'It's good you've been knocking around with her. People were saying you're a puff.'

My heart feels like it's seizing and freezing up in my chest. 'A-are they? Who's saying it? Why?'

'Everyone,' he says. 'Doesn't matter who. It's just what everyone was thinking. And come on, it seems pretty obvious in some ways.'

'Does it?' I watch him wedge another paper in a mustard-coloured door. He crosses the hall and does another one. He's torturing me, pretending his mind is on the job and not on what we're talking about.

'The important thing is that you've confused them all now. You're going about with Karen. You look like the two of you are an item, and that's good. It gives them all something else to talk about. You don't want them thinking there's something wrong with you.'

He turns and dashes up the last two flights of stairs. I toil after him, with my mind whirling round unhappily. Before I can get to the top, he's turned round, he's coming back down, and I have to follow.

Wednesday

I'm trying to revise. That means trying to remember as much as you can about everything you have learned all year at school. This is in preparation for our exams, which have been made to seem like the most important things that have happened to us in our lives since birth.

I think about Karen, at home in the old part of town, near school. Karen with her photographic memory. She won't have to do hardly any revision. She'll be in her room listening to Siouxsie and the Banshees, painting her long nails lustrous black and sticking golden stars on them. She'll be trying out new hairstyles and thinking what to write next in her ongoing, endless novel.

These are the lighter evenings and the warmer days. I'm spending them rereading and trying to make sense of all these subjects I'm supposed to know about. I've created a wall chart out of an A1 piece of card and it's a multi-coloured calendar notching off the days till the exams, telling me how many hours I have to read and relearn and revise. In this narrow room, counting off days, cudgelling my brains and watching the others play out, it's like being in prison.

I lie on my bed reading *Doctor Who Monthly*, which was delivered so late this time that I thought it was never coming. It turned up yesterday morning. The letterbox clattered just as I was about to leave for school. I leapt up and ran for it.

'You do get excited about silly things,' Mam tutted. 'It's only a comic.'

Comic! It's a *magazine!*

The cover this month has a Terileptil on. They're the new, fish-like aliens from *The Visitation*, which was a story halfway through the new season. The one where they went back in time and the Doctor caused the Great Fire of London in Pudding Lane. There's news and a comic strip and letters and reviews – and something about the *Doctor Who* exhibition opening for the summer season in Blackpool. How all the new monsters, costumes and props will be on show in exciting and dramatic tableaux.

I look up 'tableaux' in the leatherbound dictionary Mam bought me for starting the Comp.

I check my revision timetable and see that I should have done three hours on Maths tonight. And an hour on Geography, all about farming. Algebra and arable land. I'm about to get on with it when Mam's yelling from downstairs. The door's just clattered and Brian's come in late from work at his record shop. Mam's calling me downstairs.

Jacqui's coming out of her room to see what's going on. 'Hey, David,' she says, waving her paperback at me. *Stranger in a Strange Land* by Robert Heinlein. She's holding her place with her fingers and she's smoking again, which is a surprise. She has a look about her, like she's not left her room all day long. I realise that neither of us have since tea-time, stuck inside our books.

I hurry into the living room, where Brian has got the telly down from the wall unit and there are leads and cables snaking everywhere over the carpet. There's a large cardboard box open and polystyrene bits lying about. Brian is fiddling with a silver machine which sits bang in the middle of the floor. He's wiring it up and fixing it to the telly. Green lights start blinking. He presses a clunky button and a small door opens on the top.

'It's a robot,' Jacqui says. 'A droid! What about that?'

'It's a video recorder,' Mam tells me.

I stare in amazement. I've seen them at school, but no one I know has one of these in their home.

Brian strips the cellophane off a special cassette and sticks it into the machine. *Clunk, whirr, ker-chunk.* He starts to twist and fiddle with buttons and then the pictures on the telly go haywire.

'This is like the Toastie and Waffle-Maker all over again,' Jacqui chuckles, shaking her head. About a year ago, we were the first family we knew to have one of those, too. We didn't know what it was when Brian – who is mad keen on gadgets and electronics – brought it home. We made cheese toasties, banana toasties, baked bean toasties. Everything we could find in the cupboards went into toasties all one afternoon and we made ourselves sick. But we felt like we were eating something no one else could. These sandwiches were the Shape of Things to Come. Sealed round the edges crispily and melty hot inside. They were the food of the future, a time when people would *all* be slathering butter on the *outside* of their bread. We made them for my Big Nanna when she next visited and she was amazed by the Advent of the Toasties. 'Ee, you beggar! You like to keep up with the swing of things, don't you? Look at these! You do keep buying, don't you?

It's the same excitement tonight as Brian gets the TV picture to stop fizzing and keep steady. Now it seems like the video is tuned in. He doesn't say anything, though. He's like a mute magician. It's almost with a flourish that he presses down the heavy 'record' button and a red light goes on.

We watch the screen and nothing's happening. The local news. Shipyards, strikes, job losses, miners, the usual stuff. A minute goes by and we start to wonder what's so great about this.

Then he leans forward and presses 'stop', 'rewind' and 'play.'

The telly picture fizzes for a second, and clarifies. And we all give a gasp of true amazement.

'Well, well,' says Jacqui.

'Eee,' Mam says. 'Just look!'

The same thing – the exact same thing – plays again on our telly. The last minute or so runs through once more, just the same. Time travel. That's what Brian's showing us. Now we can roll back time. We can record it and roll it back and keep it for ever.

That night we make a point of walking to town for late-night grocery shopping just when *Coronation Street* starts. That show is sacrosanct, same as *Doctor Who*. We've never left the house before while it's been on. But tonight Mam trusts Brian to do the recording. We can watch it when we're back with a week's load of shopping. How swanky we feel, being out and about and knowing that our video recorder's working for us at home.

APRIL

Thursday

On that particular morning, when Jacqui falls down the stairs, it's because she is still half asleep. It's amazing it's never happened before.

She gets up in the morning and she's walking about amongst us downstairs in her night clothes, but sometimes it's almost like she's sleepwalking again, or she's only half here. Mam says her mind is still back in the book she's been reading all night in her bed sitting room. She drifts about serenely, then goes to sit in the corner of the kitchen with a mug of milky coffee. She hardly notices as Brian goes off to work, or I go off to school. She's got her nose inside a paperback and she's wordlessly setting off into her own day of reading.

Sometimes it's like Jacqui moves through a different element to the rest of us. Something slower and harder to walk through. It's still the grieving process, Mam tells me. Jacqui is learning to be a widow. But I can see Mam is a bit fed up, doing all the cooking and cleaning and shopping, when Jacqui simply goes back to bed.

She locks herself in her room and hardly helps at all.

And so the days slide by like this, and we get into a routine. It's like Jacqui's a ghost amongst us. Some days she's chatty and wants to be around us and everything is fine. Others, it's like she's pretending not to be here. She's on automatic pilot as she comes down to breakfast.

Then one day she puts a foot wrong. In her vague state, when she's at the top of the stairs, something goes wrong and she misses the step. She topples forwards. It's like her head is suddenly ten times heavier and she cartwheels down the stairs. She bounces off each step on the way. She lands in a heap at the bottom.

There are several huge crashes. Weird for such a tiny woman, is what Mam says afterwards, much later. But Jacqui doesn't cry out when she falls. That's what's so eerie about it. The noises are inhuman ones. She sounds like a wooden table or a wardrobe falling down the stairs.

Mam and I are in the kitchen. I'm having corn-flakes because it's too warm for porridge. Brian left for work twenty minutes ago. It's a quiet morning with Radio One twanging away. Then Jacqui falls down the stairs.

Mam whirls around. She's at the sink and her head whips around. She's had her hair cut much shorter. After years of it being long and straight, now it's in this short, layered look, with bits that stick up. I'm still not used to this cut, for which she splashed out and went to the unisex salon, Tint Natural, downtown. When she whirls around at the noise it's like seeing some other woman getting a shock. She looks more vulnerable somehow, and more shocked, with new hair.

We both run for the door and into the hallway.

Jacqui is lying crumpled on the carpet at the bottom of the stairs. In the instant of seeing her there, flat out cold, it is like we are hoping it will be someone else. There's only her it could be. There was only her upstairs. But the hope is there. Maybe it's some stranger lying there in our hall, unconscious.

Mam gives a strangled cry and it catches in her throat as she falls to her knees and tries to gather Jacqui up. She turns to yell at me, 'Get help! Go and get help!'

Why aren't we on the phone? 'Who'd phone us?' is what Mam always says. 'Only your Big Nanna. And who would any of us want to ring?' But this is precisely when you need a phone. 'They're handy in an emergency,' as Big Nanna says.

I grapple with the locks on the front door and hurry out to knock the neighbours up. I run in my bare feet to the blonde twins' front door, opposite ours. I bang on the rippled glass with both fists. I'm listening all the time to the noise from our hall. Mam's shouting, 'Jacqui! Jacqui!' again and again, into the old woman's face, trying to reach her.

The blonde twins' house is too slow. I dash to the next house, the one where the man looks like Hitler. I rattle the letter box, pound on the door, find the electric bell and give it a good blast.

'Jacqui, please, wake up!' Mam's voice is louder now. 'David!' she shrieks suddenly at me. 'Come here!'

I hurry back to our door. As I stand in the doorway I'm frozen, watching Mam sitting back from Jacqui. She's watching in horror as her body thrashes. It's like she's fighting Mam, making her back off. She doesn't want her near. Her limbs are jerking like a puppet's and her head has lolled forward. Her eyes are rolling back in her head.

This seems to go on for hours. We watch as she does all this weird stuff. She's in the grip of something we don't understand. Something has hold of her and we can't do anything about it as it shakes all the life out of her.

'Jacqui!' Mam calls. 'Oh, David, what are we going to do? It's Brian's Mam! What are we going to say to him?' Mam is close to tears. 'Why isn't he here?'

Then there are others standing in our hall with us. The blonde twins' mother has been brought at last by all my feverish knocking on her door. She has pulled on her housecoat and she's hurried outside. She's stepping through our open door with a grey, worried look on her face. The man Mam calls Hitler is behind her, following her into our hall.

'Phone for an ambulance,' Mam shouts at them. 'Please . . . call the ambulance out.'

Hitler goes to do as she says. The blonde twins' mother approaches and touches Mam's shoulder, just as Jacqui's fit wears off and comes to a standstill. She lies very still for a moment. She lies there stunned. Her eyes go back to normal. She seems to wake up and she looks at us all there, staring down at her in her night things.

This is when she should start glowing with a weird, unearthly light. If this is a regeneration, and she's about to turn into some other kind of Jacqui, this is when it should happen.

But none of that stuff happens. She just starts to cry, very quietly.

Later on Thursday

All that day at school is horrible and weird. Mam makes me go. There is nothing I can do at the hospital with her and Brian. I won't make it any less frightening for any of them. I won't shorten the time they have to spend there. I won't be helping anyone by missing my schooling. So I go, leaving the house at the very last minute. I have to dash down Burn Lane and through the fifties estate with only minutes to spare. There's a carpet of sticky blossom that's come down off all the trees. It's pink and thick like strawberry milkshake. I get a quick glimpse of the ambulance first, when it comes for Jacqui. I see her being loaded aboard.

I keep quiet about it all morning at school. Who is there to tell?

My tutor group in the morning always sits in the Pottery room with its wide wooden benches, smooth and pale with clay dust. The two massive kilns hum with their silver-green heat and power. Our tutor leaves the register out on his desk. He's usually off elsewhere, mumbling with the other Art teachers, or tending to his pots. It's often my job to fill in the neat columns of the register with its red ticks and blue noughts.

The other good thing about having a tutor who's an Art teacher is that he lets me use the room during lunch break. He knows how keen I am on Art. He says that, especially on days like today, when it's chilly and blustery, I can stay inside and get on with some artwork.

Today I tell Robert Woolf that it'll be OK if he comes in too. He can make something out of clay and sit in the warmth of the kiln room. He looks dubious at first but I tell him it'll be all right. I tell him about the ambulance coming for my new Nanna, Jacqui.

'Wow,' he says. 'I reckon she'll be all right, though. Sounds like she had a fit.'

A fit. It sounds so terrible.

'We thought she was dead,' I say, and Robert nods. We're both rolling out wodges of sticky clay. We're making thumb pots, just as we've both been shown in our Art classes. As we talk, we watch the kids out in the yard to the side of the Art rooms. There's an open bit with concrete shapes for kids to sit on, and a bit underneath the Languages corridor where they can shelter in the rain.

I decide I'm going to ask Robert about something that's been nagging at me. I take a deep breath.

'What you were saying, before,' I say, watching him pound out the clay, rolling it up, and pounding it out again. 'The other day, when we were going round the houses, and you were doing your paper round.'

'Hmm?'

You have to get all the air pockets out of the clay, otherwise it'll explode in the kiln. Robert is squashing and pounding it, and rolling it out again and again.

'You said I should be going out with Karen, 'cause she's a good kisser and all . . .'

'Aye,' he says, 'that's right. You should.'

I pick up my own clay again and it's gone chilly. 'You also said that I should go out with her because people say *stuff*. They say *things* about me, and this would stop them.'

'Aye . . .'

He's reluctant to look at me. Now he knows what I'm asking about, he's become awkward. He thinks I'm asking about weird stuff. He'd rather I stopped, I know.

I go on. 'Why is it they say that? Why do they?'

Robert frowns darkly. His yellow hair's all tangled in his eyes. 'Ah, don't go on about it. I shouldn't have said owt about it.'

I persist. 'But do you think I *am*?' Now I'm whispering, my voice lower than the mumbling and clicking of the hot kilns. There's no one here to listen, but my voice has gone strangled and chalky in my throat.

'I wouldn't hang around with you if I thought you were.'

But, I think, he's hanging around with me less than ever. He's only in here today, this dinner-time, because it's lashing down with rain outside. It's rare he knocks about with me at school at all.

Then he says, 'It's just that, like, a puff's not a good thing to be.'

I scald with shame at the word. It's a stupid word. A light and fluffy word. Like everything you're not supposed to be.

Then I try out a question that's been bothering me. 'But . . . what about David Bowie?'

'He was never a puff,' Robert says quickly. He's obviously thought this one through. 'And even when he went on like one, and dressed like one, in the early seventies, he was married, wasn't he? And he had a little bairn. It was all an act, a put-on, wasn't it? He was acting out a character. He was being Ziggy Stardust. All the make-up and that. He was never a real puff, was he?'

I feel betrayed by this. There's that word again. I look away. Now even David Bowie has betrayed me. And there was something about his songs that made me feel included, somehow. Like he had written them for me.

Then Robert is saying, 'You know, you can't be a puff here in a town like our town. It's just not a town that has them. Really. Have you ever seen anyone puffy round here?' He drops his voice when he says the word 'puffy'.

I think about the weird bloke who lives in the flats. Robert told me about him. How he's seen him when he delivers papers. I've never seen him. He dresses old-fashioned and looks like a creepy old man out of a horror film. He's meant to be some kind of puff, or probably one of them who interferes with kids. That's what they all say on the estate. They tell you to keep away from where he lives. He's a puff. He says good morning to people and no one ever answers.

Then I think about Mam and Brian watching TV together. Larry Grayson is on *The Generation Game*. He's funny, but I know I shouldn't laugh at anything he does or says. No one has ever told me this, but I know it's true. And anyone else who's a bit puffy on the telly. You're not meant to laugh at them. It's just not funny. Laughing at them would earn you a telling off. 'He seems like a nice man, that Larry Grayson,' Mam says. 'But he shouldn't do what he does. It's not natural, is it? It isn't nice, is it?'

That's what gets said about puffs round our house. Keep away. They mess with kids. Don't laugh, don't look, or you'll become one. And right then I know that Robert is right. It's not a good thing to be.

But . . . 'What *is* it about *me*?' I ask him. 'Why do they say it about me?'

Robert tries to explain. He won't look me in the

134

eye. 'You don't like football. You don't talk like the other lads. You don't join in. In the changing rooms, when everyone's undressing, you cover yourself up with your towel. Like you've got something different to everyone else. Like you're not the same as them. And you're bothered about your schoolwork. You like to get good marks. You like the books you read in English. You like novels with girls in. You like to paint. You never go out and hang out after school with other lads. You look too tidy. You talk about your mam. I don't know. Loads of things. It's just puffy. Puffy behaviour. You go on like a puff. People hate it. They can't stand it. They don't see why you should be like that.'

He picks up his pot again, and starts moulding and shaping it.

'Is that it?'

'You don't talk about girls.'

'Yes, I do.'

'Not about fancying them. Not about going out with them, and kissing them and stuff. You don't talk like lads do about girls.'

'Neither do you. You're the same as me.'

He looks really angry about this for a second. 'I'm not. I never was.'

'You are.'

He looks disgusted. 'I've been mates with you. But

135

you . . . I dunno. It's like you're not growing up right. Or you can't grow up in the way you should. I don't get it. Maybe you really *are* a puff.'

We carry on playing with clay. I've lost interest in it. I was going to make a Zygon-shaped thumb pot for Jacqui. All the fun's gone out of it now. I'm just squashing the clay around.

Outside the rain is drumming down steadily, harder and harder. Usually I love that noise, and the way it sounds on the flat, thin school roofs. I love the way the light turns yellow and dark. It almost feels like there's going to be lightning. Now I wish I was squirreled away somewhere, reading. I wish I could find somewhere to hide in the school and read the Nina Bawden novel we're doing in English. I squash the clay down savagely. I suppose that loving *Carrie's War* by Nina Bawden makes me a puff, too.

Then Mr Myerson the Pottery teacher comes back early from the staff room. He looks like a cross mole or something, squinting at me, and then at Robert. His hackles are up. We're messing with his precious clay. But he gave me permission, didn't he? He said it was OK. He was pleased that someone was bothered about making thumb pots and stuff.

But Mr Myerson glares blearily at Robert. 'Who's this, then? Making thumb pots in my kiln room?'

Robert freezes. He nudges me and hisses, '*Davey*. . .'

I know what he means. Get me out of this. You've got me in bother.

And I say – stupidly – to Mr Myerson, 'Well, I said he could, and—'

Mr Myerson breaks in, '*I'm* the one who says who can come into my Pottery room. Do you get that?'

And it is such a slap in the face. I should have known. Teachers can turn round suddenly and act nasty like that. They hate it when you have your own ideas. I hang my head and start clearing away my clay. I've not made anything of any use anyway. Certainly not a model Zygon I can give to Jacqui when she gets home from the hospital.

Robert squashes his thumb pot flat on the bench with his fist and he bolts out of the Pottery room. He shoots down the corridor. He goes out into the rain without a backward glance. He's looking for a footie game to get involved with before dinner hour ends. He can usually get a game anywhere, he's so good.

Thursday night

That tea-time, when I get home from school, there's this big sense of relief. Jacqui is home from the hospital. She's OK. Everyone is going on as if things are back to normal. She doesn't want fussing over. They checked out her heart and she's OK. But the weird thing is that she moves from room to room all night. She smokes and taps her ash in every room, making Brian frown. She can't get into her new novel. It's one of her favourites, too: Philip Jose Farmer, *To Your Scattered Bodies Go*. At one point she tells me that she feels unsettled. Something has made her restless and she doesn't know what it is.

'Hey, I'll be okay, though,' she adds. 'I guess that the fall knocked something loose inside my head.' I must look alarmed, because she adds, 'Not really. I feel fine.'

At one point Mam perks up with,'We've got some good news, anyway. You'll love this.'

We're all sitting on the settee, watching the telly. Jacqui's sat down at last, in her usual chair. She looks round, blinking through a blue haze of smoke.

'We're going to get a car,' Mam tells me proudly. 'Brian's been sorting it out. And it's gold, isn't it, Brian? It's a very smart one. What do you think? We'll have our own car.'

I make the right noises. I'm pretty pleased about this, actually.

'Just think,' Mam says. 'We can go shopping in Darlington, or Durham, whenever we like. No more depending on buses. We can take the car to Fine Fare to get our groceries on Friday night. It's a hatchback, too, isn't it, Brian? So we can load it up with all our shopping.'

Mam is smiling, like the whole world is opening up to us. And maybe it is. 'And holidays!' she goes. 'We can take off to the Lake District, as soon as school finishes, and when Brian's holiday starts. We can go to Blackpool to see the lights. Now, you've always wanted to see the Illuminations, haven't you?'

Suddenly all I can think about is: the *Doctor Who* exhibition on the Golden Mile in Blackpool. In the shadow of the tower. The most fantastic exhibition in the world. I feel like I would kill to see it. They always advertise it when The Show finishes. I've seen a few blurry snaps of exhibits in *Doctor Who Monthly*. And now Mam is airing the possibility that we might go there ourselves this year. In our own family car. Our golden car.

Later that night, it's time for the final episode of the new season. It's a story called *Time Flight* in which the Master has disguised himself as a green Chinaman and is taking Concorde back to the dawn of time for some reason. If I'm honest with myself, it's not very good. I still set up the portable telly in my room to record the soundtrack, even though I'm taping the pictures on video downstairs. My recordings have become very complicated, but I don't want

139

to stop making my tapes and the little covers for them. After tonight I will have a full season set.

Jacqui doesn't stay to watch the whole episode. About halfway through she gets up and wanders out of the room to sit in the kitchen, alone at the pine bench.

SUMMER TERM

Wednesday

Maybe now I'm wishing I never gave it to her. I mean, she's nice about it, the way she talks about it. I don't think Karen could ever really be nasty. Not even if she tried really hard. But as she talks about what I've given her I can tell she's trying hard to be nice. I feel myself blush and turn hot and foolish.

I have come all the way across town to where she lives. It's Wednesday night, after school. The exams are just about over now, and it felt great to nip home only briefly. It was strange not to go straight to my room to revise something else. Mam says she's pleased because I've been looking pale and too worried about my school work.

'You can do too much, you know. And that's as bad as doing too little.'

Oh no, I thought – something else to worry about.

Then she said, 'I'm glad you've got another friend. You should get out more and see your friends. Nice nights like this. When I was your age, I was hardly ever in the house.' Then she looks at me and says, 'Is this Karen your girlfriend, then?' And Mam looks embarrassed by her own question. She doesn't want to pry and yet she looks keen and somehow hurt, too, that I might have something as momentous as a first girlfriend that I haven't told her anything about.

Somehow my trip to Karen's after school on Wednesday takes on an importance that it shouldn't really have. Mam decides that I must smarten myself up. I must make a good impression on Karen's parents. So the next thing is, I'm wearing my new clothes that I got for Easter – blue cords and a short-sleeved shirt with squiggly patterns on. They smell brand new from the catalogue bags, with pins still sticking in. Mam tries to cut my hair a little straighter and shorter. Every stage in the preparations is making me more nervous and I can't even tell Mam that Karen's not my girlfriend and I don't have to impress anyone with the way I'm dressed. No one's bothered about how I look. But now, if I said so, it would hurt Mam's feelings.

I'm cleaning my new Clarks shoes in the kitchen when Brian comes in from work. Mam tells him, 'David has got a date.'

Then Jacqui appears, carrying her chess set. 'How about a game, David?'

'He's got a date,' Brian tells her.

'A date!' she gasps. 'Who with? Why does no one

keep me up-to-date with what's going on? What am I, the fragile old lady in the attic? Why don't I get to hear all the news?'

'It's not like that,' I say.

'You're meeting a girl. In your own free time. In the evening. What else should it be called?' Mam's laughing, starting on the washing up.

'So,' Jacqui says, sliding into her seat at the pine table. 'You've got a date. What are you going to do on this date?'

And at that point I hurry out of our house. It's best if I get away quickly, because I don't want to get into this. If I try to answer any more of their questions I'll get too nervous to go. I shout ta-ra from the hallway and bang the front door shut. I race off across our estate.

I'm on Burn Lane when I start torturing myself with the thought: But what if Karen thinks it's a date, too? At this point I almost get killed crossing the busy road. The car that nearly kills me roars by, horn blaring. I'm not watching properly. But . . . what if Karen thinks that, by meeting up like this, round her way, we have somehow progressed to the boyfriend-and-girlfriend phase of things. And here I am in all my stiff, immaculate, Easter things. What must that look like?

But I'm only going there as a friend. She should

know that. A really good friend. A friend she likes enough to ask around to come and sit in her room in the evening and listen to records. And to talk about our writing. This time it's my writing in particular. At last I have been brave enough to give her some pages of mine. At least, to me it seems like a brave thing to do. I put it off for as long as I could and kept reading and reading all the stuff I was given by her. But I never offered anything in return, even though I was writing the whole time.

Eventually – quite gently – she asked me again, and persisted. I kept saying I was too busy revising all my schoolwork, getting on with exam stuff. I couldn't see how I'd ever have time to do any writing. But I did. I timetabled some on my huge A1 revision chart in my room. I wanted to have some decent pages done for Karen. I wanted to have something that was well-written, that made sense and that had some kind of beginning, middle and end. Something not too rubbish and silly that I could let Karen read without fear of ridicule.

In the end – scanning through all the pages I have scribbled this spring – I settled on one little bit of story. It was about a thousand words, all about the fourth Doctor and K9 in a post-apocalyptic London, fighting radioactive mutants. I thought it was pretty good stuff – maybe a little gory. I knew I had the personality of the fourth Doctor captured exactly, and I was pleased with the banter I'd written between him and his robot dog. Very carefully I typed out this thousand words. I did it in red because the black bit of the ribbon was worn out. I had to keep starting again because of mistakes. I wanted these pages to be as tidy and perfect as possible for showing to Karen.

I left it on a thrilling cliffhanger. Hoping she would want to read on. Make me write more.

I gave the pages to her at school on Monday, as we made one of our slow circuits of the school grounds.

She'll have had time to read them by tonight, which is Wednesday. D-Day. The day of our not-date.

It's not because of any boyfriend-girlfriend thing that I feel weird. All my insides are going like a percolating coffee pot, but it's literature and not biology that's doing it. I'm just keen and frightened of hearing about my pages.

It takes me ages to find my way to her street. These old-fashioned-type houses from the nineteen-fifties have hedges around them, so it takes longer going from door to door, peering at their numbers.

At last I find it and her house is more like some kid's drawing of a house, with a chimney, a sloping roof, four windows in the corners and a door in the middle. I'm too used to our estate where everything, in comparison, is angular and futuristic. I take a breath and knock.

Her mam seems very nice and friendly, offering me a cup of tea and taking me through to their sitting room. The smell of their evening meal lingers in the air. I always find it fascinating and odd, the thought that other people are eating different stuff, and having their own routines, just as we are having ours at home. Karen's dad – who's a policeman like my dad was – is sitting in an armchair, reading the *Northern Echo*. He glances over the top of the broadsheet to say hello. He stares a bit and says abruptly, 'I knew your father.' My heart lurches a bit. Of course. Karen's dad and my dad must both have been at the station in Aycliffe together, once. 'He was a good lad.'

I'm looking down at the orange carpet. 'Thanks.'

Then Karen comes into the room to lead me upstairs. She looks very pretty, I decide. Out of school she's dressed up in her own way – a little hippyish, with earrings in and even some make-up. As I go up the stairs I'm looking at prints of views of Montmartre in Paris and, from downstairs, I can hear her dad saying to her mam, 'What, you're just letting them go up into her bedroom? You're letting her have a lad in?'

Her mam shushes him. 'It's not like that, Jack.'

The house is open-plan and I can hear them all the way up to Karen's room.

It's even smaller than my room, and it's dark and cosy. The walls are purple and she's got black-and-white photos up. 'This is my pantheon of gods and goddesses,' she says, pointing out Louise Brooks, David Sylvian, Nick Rhodes off Duran Duran. 'All the beautiful people.' She smiles, seating herself on her Indian bedspread, which is gorgeous, all beads and tiny mirrors. Strong herby-smelling incense is wafting about the room. She's got Kate Bush playing on her tape deck, wailing and whooping discordantly. 'Kate Bush is great, isn't she?' Karen says. 'I love the way she simply does what she wants. She makes the kind of music she really wants to and doesn't care about fashion or commercialism or anything else.'

I remember my dad had Kate Bush's first LP. But I think he liked her because of her leotards and her jumping about. He just fancied her, I think.

Karen smiles and nods in the direction of the pages stacked up on her desk. I recognise the blood-red typing. I saw the pages the moment I crossed the room and sat down where I was told. Karen has written on them in purple ink. Tiny, intricate hand-writing, all over each and every one of my sheets. I pick them up and squint at them, scanning the miniature notes and can't decipher them at first. My heart is bouncing along. I'm pleased that she's read my stuff, but I'm terrified at the thought of what she's going to say about them. What kind of thing was she thinking as she read?

I also feel embarrassed. This was something I enjoyed writing. I did it for myself. It isn't proper or serious at all. And yet she must have spent ages making all these notes and markings.

She watches me leafing through the pages. The sheets seem brittle, small, alien to me. Like things I've never even touched before. Now I'm ashamed of not having the right size of typing paper, and only red ink. I'm ashamed of my silly, lurid story about zombie mutants in their bombed-out city of the future. Oozing blood and green radiation everywhere, and attacking each other. I haven't even been to London before. How can I write about it? I just imagined it from seeing things on the telly and films like, One of our Dinosaurs is Missing. Karen must think I'm stupid. She'll think I'm retarded. Now I don't want to look at what she's written, so carefully and neatly in my margins.

She catches my eye, and says, 'I think you should write about something closer to home.' She looks as if she wants to be very gentle with my feelings as she says this. Like she thinks I'm going to get all touchy and upset and fly off the handle. 'All this futuristic stuff is great,' she tells me. 'And I'm sure I could never do it. Never in a million years. I don't have the imagination. But . . .' She smiles and I want to tell her: Look! I can take criticism – it's OK . . . You don't have to worry about how I'll take it. I won't cry or anything.

She takes a big breath and goes on, 'But I think this stuff' – she nods at my pages – 'it's not what you really *want* to be doing. It's not really *real*, is it?'

She sounds a bit dismissive now. *This kind of stuff. Not really real.* What does that mean?

Suddenly she reminds me of Robert Woolf. The way he's always got an opinion about things. The way he always knows what's cool or real or proper art. I nod at Karen, though, and what she's saying.

'All this stuff about *Doctor Who* is great,' she says. 'I really like it. But . . . other people write *Doctor Who* adventures, don't they? It's not really yours. He isn't your character. He doesn't belong to you.'

I frown, staring at the pages without taking them in. I'm thinking, well what about you and Duran Duran? You don't own them. You never made them up. And yet they're in all your stories. Just like Robert Smith out of The Cure. I look up and there he is, on a poster on the wall above her desk –

Robert Smith and his lopsided jammy smile and tangly hair. Then I remember: she doesn't know that I read those stories of hers. It was Robert who lent me her exercise book. I'm not supposed to know about her stories.

Karen says, 'I think you need to really think about what it is you need to write about. There's something inside of you that you need to get out. You need to put it down on paper. Otherwise it will disappear forever. You'll forget about it and you'll never know what it was. So you have to do it now. You can't let your talent down.'

I stare at her. She's got all this black mascara on and eyeshadow, just like Robert Smith himself, out of The Cure. She sits cross-legged on her peacock-blue bedspread and smiles at me. But she is so intense.

I'm stiff and embarrassed. 'Talent?'

'Of course, talent. Of course you've got talent. You're just not writing about the right things yet. You're still finding your feet and messing about.'

I fold up the pages neatly until they are small enough to fit into the back pocket of the cords I got for Easter. Karen's mam knocks at the door and she brings in a tray of tea things. The tinkly wind chimes on Karen's door sound lovely, and I decide I want some for my own room. And maybe frankincense and white musk to burn, and a bedspread like this. I don't know. There are so many things I want, suddenly. Maybe Mam would say all that stuff's too girly. But I love Karen's room. It's like a grotto. The tea her mam brings is special herbal tea – which is weird, and not like tea at all. Rose-and-raspberry flavour, and it's the most delicious thing I've ever tasted.

We sit for a while listening to The Cure and Siouxsie and the Banshees and at last I decide I had better set off home. I don't want to be walking across Burn Lane in the dark.

Karen gets up to show me out and, on the top landing she pauses and asks me in an urgent sort of voice, 'Is it true that Robert has started seeing that Julie from round his street?'

'What?' I don't know anything about this. And why is Karen asking me about him?

'Someone was saying he's started going out with this girl in the third year. Julie someone. She lives quite near him.'

'I haven't heard.' I find that I'm just about whispering to her. 'But I haven't seen much of Robert while the exams have been on.'

Karen nods. 'I hope he's not seeing her. They say this Julie lass is a bit horrible. She's proper slack.'

'Slack' is an awful word. I've heard girls in our school use it about each other quite a lot. It means they hang around with lads too much. It means that they'll do anything with them. I've never heard Karen use the term before. It sounds strange coming from her, like she is using someone else's language. She says to me, 'Let me know if you hear anything. If he tells you anything about . . . going out with this Julie.'

And I realise that Karen is still keen on Robert. But it's ages since the beginning of the school year, when they were going out. Robert has just about forgotten it. All he remembers is that Karen is a good kisser, or so he says.

'All right,' I tell her – though I don't really want to know what he's got to say about this Julie at all. And then I head downstairs, say good night to Karen's parents in their sitting room, and hurry out into the street, wishing we lived in an open-plan house.

Friday

At the end of this week our new car arrives.

As promised, it's gold and it sort of glimmers in the sunshine as it sits there in front of our house. Brian goes round it, polishing its bodywork with a rag. It's a hatchback. Mam said what it was called, but I've forgotten. The hatchback means that there's plenty of room for when we go away on trips and journeys. We can throw everything we need in the back. We can take as much as we like, because it is so spacious.

Tonight – filled with thoughts of the Lakes and the attractions of Blackpool – we set off in our new gold car. We drive to the town precinct and park at the very top of the multi-storey at the back of Fine Fare.

Just because we can.

We load up with the week's groceries – a whole week's at once! – and push our trolley up the bending, sloping ramp, to load our stuff straight into our hatchback's boot.

Sunday

'Are you courting yet? Your mam says you are . . . !'

This is my Big Nanna as we perch in her living room on Sunday.

'You want to watch out though, with these girls. You start going about with girls and they'll have all your money off you. You have to buy things for them and they want to be going out all the time.'

'I'm not courting . . .' The word feels silly and old-fashioned as I say it. I am aware of everyone's eyes on me.

My Big Nanna's living room is very warm. It always is. She has the gas fire turned up full when she has visitors and by the end of the afternoon you're dropping off. She brings in plate-loads of squashy butterfly cakes sprinkled with icing sugar and dollopped with jam; Victoria sponge bursting with fresh cream; dainty little sandwiches crammed with red salmon and cucumber. And cup after cup of tea.

Mam's looking at me. 'I don't think it's courting, really. He's too young. It's just a nice friend he's got –

isn't it, David? But, do you know what? They write letters to each other. Long letters, pages thick, they come in the post every other day. Even though they live on the same town. Even though they both go to the same school.'

'Ee! Wasting money on stamps,' Big Nanna laughs. 'Really though, you don't want to get too serious, our David. You should have lots of different friends at your age. You shouldn't be getting serious about one particular girl. That only leads to trouble. You're too young.'

Here, Big Nanna makes the mistake of looking sideways at my mam.

Of course, Mam thinks it's Big Nanna having a dig at *her*. And, of course, Big Nanna *is*.

'They start too young these days. You can ruin your whole young life. You want to slow down. Grow up slower. You spend a long time grown up, you know. Don't be in a rush to get there.'

I nod and smile through most of this. I'm trying to fix on the telly, which blares away in the corner. But it's football – tuned to the highlights for Brian and my Uncle Peter, who lives with Big Nanna. So I end up staring at the army of ornaments on Big Nanna's fireplace. Brass animals and souvenirs of her travels around the world – German beer mugs and African statuettes.

'David is sensible,' Mam says pointedly. 'He won't be getting into any trouble.'

Big Nanna nods, giving Mam another sidelong glance along the settee. 'They don't know what they're doing at that age, do they? They don't know that they can spoil their whole future, easy as anything.'

I'm starting to blush. I know what they're really talking about. They are sitting either side of me on the settee, and talking over my head.

Mam was sixteen when she was pregnant with me. My Big Nanna threw her out. She had to live with my dad's family. That's what's really being talked about here. The dangers.

'David's not daft,' Mam says. 'He's not like the rest of them. And he's not like his dad.'

We all flinch at the mention of Dad. Then Big Nanna looks cross that Mam has brought him into their conversation. 'Aye, well. He'd better not turn out like his dad, eh?'

Mam grits her teeth. 'The bairn's dad was all right at the beginning. He was devoted to me – and to David.'

Now I can see that Brian looks uncomfortable. Mam carries on, though. 'It was the police force that turned him. I think they go a bit funny on the Force. A bit strange.'

'They go on daft,' Big Nanna says. 'Like they think they're coppers off the telly. *The Sweeney* and all that lot.'

'It's no good for family life,' Mam sighs. 'But at the start he was lovely. He could never do enough for us. And he loved David, of course. He was a good dad.'

They go quiet for a while, as the men watch the football.

Then Mam is saying, 'David won't get into any kind of trouble.'

'You don't know. Lads. The way they go on.'

'Not David,' Mam says.

'You reckon he was going round this lass's house.'

'They write stories together,' Mam sighs. 'That's all they do. They're just friends.'

My Big Nanna purses her lips. 'Friends,' she says scornfully, like there's no such thing. Especially between the sexes. Suddenly, as I turn to look at her, her whole view of things seems written on her face. The world is a frightening place; a savage, primordial land where everyone wants to have sex with everyone else and get everyone pregnant and there's nothing more to life. Apart from housework and drudgery, which is big on Big Nanna's list, too.

She thinks that growing up and being a teenager is like white-water rafting. A series of tumultuous hazards. And maybe it is. But – despite all her fears –

and the fears that I can see she is passing on to my mam – I don't feel like I'm swimming along through rapids and hazards. Not yet, anyway. And, if I'm honest, I don't think I'll ever be all that keen on braving those waters.

What if I said to them, right now, over the noise of their barbed chatter, and the background murmur of Sunday football, 'Actually, I don't like girls. Not in the way you think. Not in the way you expect and assume. I'm never going to do any of the things you are scared of. No one will get pregnant. You won't have another early marriage to arrange. You won't have some new daughter-in-law to hate. There'll be none of them upheavals. Nothing like that from me. So stop it. Just stop worrying and going on about it. You don't know anything. I don't like girls.'

I don't like girls.

And even though I don't shout this out, I'm shocked that I've even thought it inside my head.

My ears are ringing, even though I haven't said a word.

I have shocked myself.

But it's true. It's all true.

JUNE

Tuesday

'My mam reckons you're paranoid about *Doctor Who.*'

The way Robert says this makes me flinch. It is so casual and so sudden. He says it with a light sneer, turning round in the magazine section of WHSmiths, where he is flicking through a body-building magazine. The two of us have come to Darlington for an afternoon of mooching about. Of course WHSmiths is our first stop. I am checking out the newest releases upstairs in Books.

'They've got *The Leisure Hive*, brand new this month,' I say, showing him my prize. My heart is thumping. 'There are two copies. So we can buy one each.' In my hand I've got my counted-out money, ready for the cashier. I know I've got just enough and already I'm imagining myself racing through the book on the bus back to our town.

But Robert looks at me then with a weary shake of his head. He's got his earring in and it's a little silver dagger jiggling in one lobe. And, now that I look at him properly, he's got a bit of black eyeliner and mascara on. His sister's helped him with his Goth make-up for coming out to Darlington. 'Look,' he tells me, waving his magazine. 'I'm not really bothered about the new *Doctor Who* book. I've got too many as it is. Ones I've never even read.' He shrugs. Tuts at me.

'What does your mam mean, "paranoid"?' I ask. How can he not want a copy of *The Leisure Hive*? I scan through the opening pages. It smells of new book. And it begins quite differently to the TV version. The first chapter is written from somebody's point of view – a deck chair attendant on Brighton beach. It is weird, funny, immediately absorbing. I snap it shut and clasp it to my chest. Save it till later. I look at Robert, thinking how strange it is that he's no longer saying, 'The Show'. He keeps saying '*Doctor Who*', out loud and boldly. It's somehow belittling The Show. Somehow it makes me feel superstitious.

He tuts at me again. 'You know what "paranoid" means.'

'Like everyone's out to get you?'

'No,' he shakes his head. 'That isn't what it means. "Paranoid" means you can't think about anything else. All you've got in your head is *Doctor Who*. That's it.'

I frown. I feel a stab of betrayal. A squirm of embarrassment. But I also feel cross that he – or his mam – has got the word wrong. I am sure of it. I hate to be accused of the wrong thing.

I'm blushing as we queue at the till. Robert's first, scooping out change for his body-building magazine. Then I count out my money once again, and watch the girl put *The Leisure Hive* into a paper bag. As we leave, I say to Robert, 'I think your mam means "obsessed". The word your mam means is "obsessed". You can say someone is obsessed with something. But not paranoid. You could even say they were paranoid about being thought of as obsessed with something. But you can't – I can't – be paranoid about *Doctor Who*.'

Robert tuts. We head out to Queen Street, which pulses with traffic and noise and pedestrians. I have to hurry to keep up with him as he stalks along, bearing towards the market and the alternative shops in the hidden-away streets. Hippy shops and Gothy shops: they are what's next on our agenda. Maybe I'll buy some incense. I won't be able to burn it in my room, but it'll smell nice anyway.

There's tall, newly-muscled, mascara-wearing, bored-sounding Robert Woolf tutting at me. He doesn't even want me here, tagging along. We look at studded belts and skull-and-crossbone rings. We look at obscure-sounding records and strange posters.

He doesn't say much to me. I can see he's bored with me, with *Doctor Who*, with Terrance Dicks and with being twelve. He is bored with being in Darlington on a Saturday afternoon. He wants to be on the Left Bank in Paris or Greenwich Village in New York, where everyone is hip, artistic, *eclectic*. Here everyone is togged up in anoraks, even though it's nearly summer. They bustle along, pear-shaped northern people, thinking about boring and tut-worthy stuff. I know he knows no one's thinking about really important things. It's all trivial. And here comes Robert, his mind seething with the meaning of life and sex and death and everything.

I'm happy, though. Even if he'd rather be on his own. I've got my new *Doctor Who* book. A thin, floppy paperback, spanking new. That friendly neon logo. Another new world. Argolis. Radioactive world of gangster lizards and tachyon technology. Now I'd be just as happy to go home and start reading it. If Robert decides he doesn't want me about any more I could just get on a bus myself and return home. I'll read my new book in two hours and then read it again. And maybe Jacqui will be interested in borrowing it. No sign of me or Jacqui losing our interest in The Show, the novels based on The Show, or Terrance Dicks.

As I watch Robert trying on Goth belts and

leather necklace things in these gloomy shops where there's heavy, dirgey music playing, I'm wondering if this is what it's like when you start to become a teenager properly. Is this what happens? Is this a typical teenage thing? You lose your interest in things you really care about. You change. You are never the same again. Here in Darlington, heads throbbing with nasty, thumpy, Gothy music, we're both witnessing Robert metamorphosing into something older, weirder, and less happy.

It's this thought that lodges in my head for the rest of the day. All the way back across Darlington town centre, in the bus queue and during the journey home, I feel faintly sick with dread at the thought that you have to change. Because things always change. And people seem to accept the changes gladly. They even look forward to the changes. But you will never be the same again. There is no going back to who you were. 'You'll see what it's like when you get older,' Mam has told me. When you're a teenager this, and when you're a teenager that. 'You'll feel differently then. It all changes round. Your hormones. You grow. You change. You'll be a different person then.'

Is that how Jon Pertwee felt? The Third Doctor lying there on the laboratory floor? When he was fatally irradiated by the Spider Queen from Metebelis

Three. And he was suffused by that curious glowing mass of energy. And he started to change. He started to regenerate. Did he think, Oh no, now I have to change forever, I've got to be the fourth Doctor now and become completely different. A whole new person. And did he resent that? Was he scared? He had no choice, of course. And now the fourth Doctor has gone as well and now we have a fifth Doctor and so it goes on.

When we get back to our town, Robert sort of dismisses me. 'Yeah, see ya,' he says, when we get off the bus, and then he wanders back to his place.

SUMMER HOLIDAYS

Black Swan Caravan Park,
Lake Coniston, Lake District

Dear Karen,

The eighteen Pot Noodles were a mistake. We're all agreed on that. It's what we're all thinking, and it's only Tuesday. Whose idea was it? We can't remember. We don't know who to hold responsible. We all saw the adverts for Pot Noodles on the telly. One of us – maybe it was Mam? – said that they seemed like the ideal thing for us to take on holiday for our supplies. They are quick and delicious, convenient, nutritious and all you need is a kettle of boiling water. We should at least have tried one first, before bulk-buying.

Last Friday we bought eighteen with our weekly Fine Fare shop. Enough to last the three of us each evening of our holiday in the luxury caravan. Last night was our first night and we tried our first Pot Noodle. We each had Sweet and Sour. And we all hated them. Mam put down her fork, saying, 'I can't eat this muck every night.' The cupboard in the galley kitchen is filled with the things. We have to think again. Tonight we're going to get fish and chips in Coniston.

So that's our first – and hopefully only – disaster here on holiday in the Lakes. Everything else has been OK. The drive was all right and the roads weren't too busy. We listened to Mam's favourites, to the Eagles and Dr Hook all the way, though. Our caravan park is hidden away in the hills around Lake Coniston. It's shaded and surrounded by huge fir trees, and everything has that pine needle scent, like Christmas or toilet cleaner.

Luckily our caravan is really luxurious, just like the brochure promised. There's a sitting-room area at the front, with windows staring out at the rest of the park and the blue mountains beyond the lake. We haven't been down to the Lake yet. Too busy sorting everything out, and trying out Pot Noodles and trying to make ourselves at home. Mam's even been round with the duster and the ewbank (the carpet sweeper thing), liking everything to be just so. Anyway, I thought I'd drop you a line to tell you how we're getting on. How are you?

Already our town seems a million miles away. We've been away just over twenty-four hours, but it's like being in a different world now. It feels in a way like we've always been living in a luxury caravan with blue mountains around us. I'm hoping I've brought enough books with me – three Terrance Dicks, three Malcolm Hulkes, a Nina Bawden, two Roald Dahls, two John Christophers, a Mary Norton, an E. Nesbit and a Barbara Euphan Todd.

I've brought lots of paper, too, because I want to write.

Dear Karen,

I wonder what you're doing. You never said what you'd be getting up to in the holidays. Same as me, I suppose. We like more or less the same things, don't we? Trouble is, with the things I do, it looks like I'm just sitting there. 'Get out and play! Run around! Get some air!' Mam says. If you're sitting there reading or writing away in the corner, you're concentrating and probably frowning. That doesn't look as if you're enjoying yourself. Not enough. 'Look at the weather out there! It's glorious! Get out there and soak up some sun!'

I've bought a clip-on sun visor to go over my glasses, because all the bright sun irritates my eyes. But now my glasses feel like heavy goggles and leave red weals down my nose. But it's better than squinting everywhere, because that makes me look unhappy, too, apparently.

I've discovered I like to read in the sun. Maybe in

a patch of dappled shade. That's best. There's a bit of beach halfway along Coniston, just down the hill from our caravan park. We've been a couple of times already and it's marvellous, like being somewhere really exotic. We walked down on our second day and followed some of the others from our park: our new neighbours, though no one talks. They were lugging picnic baskets and rolled-up blankets and towels. It takes a good walk through scrubby sand dunes and a bit of forest, and then there's all these swampy rushes and wooden bridges over dried-up, cracked lagoon things. We stopped to watch dragon-flies zizzing and flitting about – silver and purple and bright emerald. And then there's all these rocks and pale sand, and it's a perfect beach stretching for half a mile or so.

Even first thing in the morning there are dozens of holiday people out there, claiming their patch and staring at the dazzling, choppy waters of the lake. We sit here for hours, in the small patch our family have staked out. We bring bags with sandwiches and bottles of pop and everything we'll need for a full day in the sun. Mam's happy sunbathing. She loves the sun. She still thinks I should be running about more and enjoying myself. Other kids are dashing into the lake, splashing about, even swimming to and fro. They are getting in boats and sculling up and down.

Waving to their parents on the shore. Actually, Mam wouldn't be that keen on me doing that. Wouldn't trust me not to drown myself.

Dear Karen,
Being away makes you think about home. I'm thinking about my room in our house. There I've got incense burning (though Mam's not happy about me messing with matches). I have books piled on my desk and along the walls. And it's there that I sit instead of watching endless TV downstairs. I'm starting to write seriously, I think. I think I'm doing what you suggested. I'm writing about things I actually know about. Things I've experienced.

Now I've got my own record player in my room, too. Most of my records are old kids' ones, though. Disney songs and stuff like that. I've a few doublers, though, donated to me when Mam and Brian brought their two record collections together, and discovered they had more than one copy of things like Rod Stewart's *Atlantic Crossing*. So now I've got that. On the cover, a sci-fi Rod with neon pink legs, stepping over the Atlantic like a Martian out of *War of the Worlds*.

They had Rod Stewart playing the night they had the house-warming party at ours. Last year, it was, before Brian's dad died. We moved to our new estate to be closer to his parents, and to be away from the house we'd shared with Dad.

They had all their records on that night. Fleetwood Mac, Bob Dylan, the Beatles.

It's rare that we have people round our house. Downstairs that night there was adult conversation. The hubbub of the few neighbours they had already met. Brian's mam's two sisters, who were visiting the UK, yammering away in fast New Yorkese. We could hardly understand them at first.

Upstairs, listening hard and longing to be a part of their visit and this party, I could smell all the delicacies Jacqui's sisters had prepared and carried over the street on trays covered with cool tea towels. It turned out they ran their own patisserie in Brooklyn, and that's where the two sisters had grown up and learned to bake, so many years ago. The smells were wonderful. Cinnamon, nutmeg, ginger. The special breads and cakes. The vanilla cream of the custardy cakes. The tang of alcohol was weird in our house, where no one ever drank or smoked. Mam was letting Brian's mam and dad puff away on their duty-free tabs in our living room. The yellow smoke came curling up our stairs, for me to sniff as I sat there at the very top. I watched the smoke turning newly-painted Artex and white plaster yellow. The paint of our new council house was curdling with the nicotine. Everything was turning old overnight. Worn in by our house-warming party.

Mam has some kind of secret sense. A special power thing. She knew I was still awake. She knew I was hanging about listening at the top of the stairs. In my slippers.

'Look at the time! It's half past midnight!' She's laughing as she scurries up the stairs towards me. She looks bright and strange to me, in her party make-up. She's wearing a long dark skirt Jacqui's sisters brought her as a present. She clenches handfuls of fine printed fabric as she comes up the stairs.

'You can come down and say goodnight to everyone.' And now I have to face them all, standing there in my pyjamas. A shy kid. Brian's new kid, the one he has taken on as his own.

Last the Whole Night Long is playing. James Last's party record – the one with the glass of bubbly on the front. As the endless orchestral medley plays, I stare at the adults in our living room at midnight. They are all looking bleary-eyed and happy. The neighbours, the New York aunties, and Brian's mam Jacqui, and Arnold, his dad. His dad looks happy – even though we all know he is ill. Raising his glass of whisky and his tab end in the same hand. They've even got their old spaniel sitting by our fake fire, next to the Snoopy Mam won.

I'm staring at them having a good time and I'm thinking: This is how adults carry on when your back is turned.

Dear Karen,
After that party at ours, Brian's mam Jacqui went back to America for a visit with her sisters. She was away for a while – over a month – and, during that time, their dog died. It was awful.

At six in the morning, Brian's elderly dad, Arnold, walked over to knock on our door. He was distraught and in his stockinged feet. 'The pup's gone,' he said. Mam and Brian had to deal with it all. She phoned the council and they said you either have to chuck the body on the tip, or dig down four feet in the garden. They did, and it was winter and hard work. Their garden was tiny. It was a grisly business, she said. I came down to breakfast that morning and Mam told me that the dog was dead. I said, 'You're kidding', and she said, 'Why would I joke about a thing like that?'

Then it wasn't long before Arnold himself became very ill. Mam took matters into her own hands and went down town and telegrammed Jacqui in New York to come home at once. When she turned up, not long after, Jacqui was so upset she tore a strip off Mam: 'Ruining my visit like that.' She'd been having a wonderful time, back in the city where she'd grown up. Walking in the snow in Central Park, she'd been to Dog Hill, where dog walkers let their pets go free for a run, even though they weren't meant to. Weirdly – she told me afterwards – she'd had a premonition, up on Dog Hill, standing there in the snow with her sisters and their terriers – that things weren't good at home. She knew something was up with the pup, and with her husband. Jacqui thought she could stay there, in the city that she was learning to feel at home in again, and forget about problems in England. She spent her days in the galleries of the Met and MOMA and her evenings seeing shows with lots of singing and dancing on Broadway, but she knew she'd have to come back sooner rather than later.

Jacqui never cried at the state of Arnold, as he neared death. Mam said maybe it was the professional calm of the ex-nurse. 'I wasn't a nurse,' Jacqui snapped at her in the hospital. 'I was a dental hygienist.'

Mam and Brian went back and forth to the hospital to see him. I remember them bringing back *The Empire Strikes Back* chewy sweets from the hospital shop. When Arnold died, it was the middle of the day. I was at school, and Mam and Brian raced to the hospital in a taxi to see him. They were just too late.

A nurse said to Mam, 'You've missed him by five minutes.' Apparently it was like he had driven off in a taxi, the way she said it.

The one time Jacqui cried, Mam said, was in all the preparations for the funeral tea at their house. She had asked Mam how to go about making one of those Bird's trifles, the ones that come in packets with the hundreds and thousands sprinkled on top . . . and there were finger buns to do, and a corned-beef pie to make and . . . Her sisters would have had the buffet done in a flash. They could bake anything. They were experts. Why weren't they there to help her? This was the worst moment of her life. Mam told Jacqui to go for a lie-down and she would see to it all. And Mam did, she told me. She made pastry and breads and pies and trifles. Everything she could think of. She worked for hours on end in Jacqui's kitchen, sending Brian off to the corner shop for further supplies of flour and brown sugar and things like ground almonds, vanilla essence and jam. Mam says it's easier, when times are hard, to throw yourself into an activity like this.

I went round there, to Jacqui and Arnold's house, and it was odd, going to someone else's home rather than our own after school. Adults were milling about in black, talking and eating. I sat on a pouffe, where I'd always sat when I was round Arnold and Jacqui's, reading *Doctor Who and the Image of the Fendahl.* It was very smoky round there. One of the reasons I liked to go to their house had been for the smokiness and the chat: Arnold and Jacqui would talk to me properly, like another grown-up. Just like my dad's family used to. The smoky grown-up talk was the same.

It wasn't long after the funeral that they decided that the best thing would be if Jacqui left the house she had shared with Arnold, gave it back to the council, and moved in with us, in our new house in Hampton Place. There was the very narrow spare bedroom between the two main bedrooms, hardly bigger than a cupboard, but she was welcome to it.

She read novels all through the night. Have I told you this before, Karen? The bedroom doors in our house have little windows above them, and the light spills on the landing. I'm not allowed to leave my light on late, but Jacqui was. She read *Gone with the Wind* and *The Mallen Streak*. Back then, last year, we all got our books, each Saturday, from The Big Book Exchange on the North Road in Darlington. (We stopped going when Mam realised it was a sex shop in the back.)

Sorry, Karen. You asked me to write about real-life stuff. And I write about dead people and sad stuff like this. I'm sorry!

Dear Karen,

Here's a scene from just last month. I'm trying to write it more or less as it was. It's about what happened to Brian's mam and how she stopped living with us. It starts with Mam shouting in the upstairs hallway.

'Don't you think you owe him an apology?'

Mam's voice is harsh, out on the landing. She sounds brittle, angry and loud. I've never heard her sound like that before.

This was on a Monday tea-time. Upstairs in our house. I was reading in my room. Was it me that Mam was shouting at from the hallway? I could tell how angry she was because she was talking so precisely.

'Don't you think you're going to hurt his feelings? Have you even thought about that? Do you ever think of anyone else but your own self?'

Then it clicks. She is shouting at Jacqui, who is sitting quietly in the middle, narrow bedroom, which by now has been her home at ours for a number of months. She moved in and she's a new member of our household. We've all got along fine. She plays chess with me and stays up late drinking strong coffee and trying not to smoke fags. She sits up reading all night. She is in mourning, Mam has told us. We have to tiptoe around Brian's mam. Her feelings are still very raw and bruised. Her nerves are close to the surface. Brian's dad hasn't been buried long.

Jacqui seems cheerful enough. Getting rid of their council house. Putting their heavy furniture in storage. Occasionally cooking us exotic meals, like Jewish stuff. She is American and therefore familiar-seeming in some ways but, in others, completely unfathomable. Mam says Brian is rather like his mam. You can't tell what he's really thinking either. Mam liked Brian's dad, Arnold, because he treated Mam like the daughter he never had.

And now, this. Jacqui has announced – out of the blue – that she is no longer happy with us. She wants to return to New York City, to be with her sisters. To be where she grew up as a young woman. She always intended to go back there. Arnold never wanted to, but now things are different. Circumstances have changed. I can hear her patiently explaining to Mam. There is nothing to tie her to us or this place any more.

When Jacqui talks, I crane to listen at the wall. Her room is filled with heavy cushions and tapes-tried rugs on the walls and floor. Her voice with its burbling accent is muffled, but I can still hear the weariness in her voice, 'I don't wanna hurt Brian's feelings. Of course I don't, Mary. He's my son.'

183

'Hah,' Mam shouts. It sounds so weird to me. She's never raised her voice to Jacqui before. It's kind of exciting, too. 'How do you think Brian feels? He's made you welcome here, in his home. In our home. We've all made you welcome here. Me, Brian, and the bairn. We've made room for you and we've all been getting along . . .'

I hear Jacqui sigh dramatically. 'I don't wanna talk about this now, with you.' She says, 'witchoo.' I can just picture her, sitting in her basket chair at the foot of her bed and gazing wistfully at her bookshelves. Wanting Mam to leave her alone and this confrontation to be over. Jacqui must have thought it no big deal, just announcing to Mam that she was going to leave. The news has obviously gone down really badly.

'I don't care what you want,' Mam snaps back. 'You can't just treat us like this. Like a bloody hotel.'

'I want to go back to the States. That's it. My sisters are there, as you know, Mary. I left a whole life back there, years ago. It'll be a better life there for me now. Now that I haven't got Arnold anymore. There just isn't anything for me here.'

'Nothing!' Mam yells. 'What about Brian? Your son?'

'He's got you and David. I'm not part of this.'

'You've got a family here. You've said that David's

184

like a grandson to you. How's he going to feel? When are you going to tell him you're just upping sticks and leaving us? Will you tell him like you told me? All matter-of-factly, like going right across the ocean is some everyday thing?'

'I'll explain to him,' Jacqui says heavily. 'Of course I will. But . . . he's not my grandson really, is he? Not really.'

A small pause. 'We've been like a family,' Mam says, quieter now. 'Brian has accepted David like his own child. Brian supports us. He's like a dad to David. Me and Brian, we're as good as married.'

'But still,' says Jacqui. 'My real family is elsewhere. I wanna be back with my sisters. In my own city. Not in this tiny town. This estate. This little room. I don't wanna end my days here, like this.'

Mam can't believe it. 'What have they got in America that we haven't got here?'

I know that Jacqui is looking at Mam, amazed. I know, because Jacqui has told me things about New York. She's told me about sitting in the park with a picnic and papers and books to read, with all the tall shining buildings standing protectively over you. And about going to the swanky restaurant on top of the World Trade Centre. And about the life-sized dinosaurs in the Natural History Museum. And the flashing, glamorous brilliance of the theatres on

Broadway. The paintings in the galleries. The honking of taxis on the streets and the raucous music everywhere and the tempting aromas of a thousand nationalities cooking their different dinners at all times of the day and night. Jacqui's told me about the history of the place and the atmosphere. I know that it's the most wonderful, magical and splendid place.

'It's my home,' she tells Mam again, quietly. 'I just wanna go home now.'

Funny, writing down just what they said. Don't things sound awful when you read them back? Maybe I should stop doing this writing-from-life thing.

Dear Karen,
I'm definitely going to stop this writing-from-life thing.

Mam found and read my pages. Everything I've written this year. She and Brian have been through it all, looking for bits about themselves.

'All this stuff. It's horrible. It's like you're holding us up to ridicule. Brian's not happy at all. He's furious with you. How could you do that, David? Write all that stuff down and make fun of us all. How do you think that makes him feel? You are as important as I am to him, even though you aren't his. And all the sacrifices we have made for you and all the things you want. You've flung it all back in our faces.

Do you ever hear Brian complain? We give you everything, and this is how you repay us. You make him look like an idiot. You write all this sneaky stuff. What are people going to think about that? You've made us sound common. You've made all of us sound downright awful. All our family secrets, everything. I could have died of shame when I saw what you've been writing. How dare you scribble things down and hide them away like some nasty sneak? How dare you even dream about sending these things in the post to that girl?'

Dear Karen,
Because we're not eating all of those Pot Noodles, we were in Coniston last night – the little town, I mean, rather than the lake. We were picking up a few things in the supermarket there and, when we came out, we were just about to cross the road to the car park when Mam saw something and dashed off.

There was a girl, just up the road, trying to cross the road. She looked about thirteen and she was walking stiffly. Her limbs were moving spasmodically and she was having trouble keeping in line. Mam had seen her first and she was hurrying over to her. Me and Brian stood there, surprised, as Mam went over. She took hold of the girl very gently and lead her firmly over the road.

Then she came back and we went to our car. She never said anything until we were underway, heading home to our caravan. 'That's how I was when I was thirteen. It was the year I learned to walk again.'

I ask her, 'What was it? What was wrong with you?'

Mam turns to smile at me. 'I don't know what it was. But I stayed off school for a whole year. I was in the house by myself much of the time. Your Big Nanna was out at work, cleaning. We never found out what it was. But I learned to walk again, eventually.'

We absorb this knowledge quietly, as Brian drives us back towards the lake in the late sunshine. We swerve along the winding roads and they are almost all covered over by the overhanging trees.

That night, as Mam cooks dinner on the tiny stove and we eat at the small table, I'm thinking of her being thirteen – just a bit older than me – and trapped in the house. Her limbs jerking about like that girl's. Shaking and trying to keep still. Something inside me goes cold when I think of it. Like when I think of anything bad happening to Mam. I look at her, and Brian, and imagine awful things, and it feels like all my insides turn over inside of me.

We have Vesta Chow Mein and it's one of my

favourites. One of the earliest things I remember eating. Mam and me would have special exotic food nights – years ago,way before Brian was on the scene. She would fry up the crispy noodles till they puffed up fat and golden. She'd snip open the silver packet of soy sauce and spice up the hot soft noodles and the peppery sauce. Tonight the caravan is filled with the fragrant steam of the Orient.

After eating we take an evening walk down to the lake, where the air is soft. The lake is smooth and silvery purple under the evening sky. It's almost time to go home. We're all quiet about this, but we know we're going back to our town soon, and the peacefulness of this holiday will shortly be at an end. There's been something so still about these days. They have been so long and undisturbed. I've loved finding my own place on the shingle beach, hidden away in the small bay, and sitting propped against a tree trunk. I've been reading books Mam says she thinks are really girls' books and probably too young for me – *Carrie's War* again, and *Mrs Frisby and the Rats of Nimh*. This last one, about the mother of a family of mice who does everything she can to save her young family from the farmer and the rats. She lives in a cosy home under the ground beneath a brick – and the book is about her having to move house because the field is about to be ploughed. One of her sons is sickly and unwell, but Mrs Frisby is brave and manages to save him and all the others. I bought the book in the gift shop in Coniston, the day I officially ran out of novels from home. I found it on the paperback carousel and remembered how we'd read it in Junior School. Back then it was just a novel about mice, with lots of adventure and danger in it. Now I'm finding more meanings.

I do that – I read books and think: that's like him, or that's like her. I'm looking for things I recognise in everything I read. I want to feel at home in these books I pick up. I want them to be more familiar than home and ordinary life. I think that's because I can pick them up and carry them with me. I always have the safe dimension of the book to escape into. Books are bigger on the inside than on the out, just like a police box.

That night we sit down at the little beach on Coniston that has become our favourite bit. We are there until it's almost dark, which makes walking back over the rushy dunes quite difficult. But we sit as long as we can, watching the water.

It's the end of the first holiday we have taken as a family. And just now we really feel like a family. Even if Brian is quiet, tossing rocks into the lake, trying to make them skip. Mam's in a world of her

own, probably thinking about that girl and her trem-
bling arms and legs, teaching herself to walk again.

But this is us, anyway. At the end of our holiday.
Sitting on the beach of the lake, and thinking that
it's time to go home.
Love,
David.

OCTOBER – BLACKPOOL WEEKEND!

Saturday, early afternoon

'I wish we'd never brought your friend,' Mam says, with one of her sighs.

Robert Woolf is in the toilets of the café at Forton Services. He's trying to get the sick out of his jeans and T-shirt.

'That's what you get for being selfish, you see,' Mam says. 'Did he offer any of us a sweet? No, he ate the whole packet himself. And this is what you get.' She pulls a terrible face. 'Ooh, I can still smell it. The car will reek of it. It'll make us *all* throw up.'

Mam and I are sitting at a table in the services' restaurant, drinking cups of milky tea. Forton Services has a brilliant restaurant because it is a flying saucer shape, sitting on top of a white futuristic tower. It looms over the M6 and all the traffic whizzing along north and south. Around us there are miles and miles of greeny-grey, soggy-looking fields. We've been on the road for almost two hours so far, so we needed a break.

'Poor Brian,' Mam says, reflectively dunking a biscuit in her tea. 'He's got all this driving to do, and there he is, scrubbing out his new car. Cleaning up some kid's sick. Not even from his own kid.' She frowns again. 'I can still smell it. Fudge. What was his Gran doing, giving him fudge to eat on a car journey?'

Mam's right about Robert's greed. He didn't offer any fudge to anyone else and he started eating it straight away, before we'd even got out of our estate.

'I reckon it's excitement that's made him sick,' I tell Mam. 'As well as eating a whole bag of fudge.'

She smiles at me. 'Excitement? About Blackpool?'

Of course! We've been waiting for this and planning this for weeks. Saving money, organising cameras and film. Researching all the attractions of the place. Plotting and planning our day-trip. And dreaming about the *Doctor Who* exhibition opposite the Central Pier, bang in the middle of the Golden Mile and in the shadow of Blackpool Tower. This is where we are going at last. I can feel my own stomach churning now, thinking of it again as we sit in the flying-saucer restaurant above the motorway.

It's as if we're going to meet the Doctor himself. How will we feel, come the early hours of the morning, when we're driving back the other way, back home from Blackpool? What will we have seen?

How fantastic a time will we have had? It's a whole city built for having pleasure in. Everything about it will be amazing, fantastic, luminously brilliant! And there's a whole exhibition about *Doctor Who*. An underground place where The Show comes to life. Where thinking about The Show and everything in it is the norm.

Robert comes slouching back from the toilets, looking damp and shame-faced. Even his yellow hair looks damp, as if he's had to wash fudge-vomit out of that, too. He has a splash of pure white at the front of his fair hair. He did it with a paint brush and Domestos, to see what would happen. It looks quite good, really. Now his whole face is that pale, as he comes to sit with us and has a sip of tea.

Mam looks at him and decides it's best not to go raking over the rights and wrongs of eating a whole bag of fudge in the back of the car straight after lunch. I can see she's concerned about Robert now. She is his surrogate parent today. She has to look after him. 'Are you all right, pet?'

He takes the cup of tea she offers him.

He still smells sicky, though, I think. I hope he's not spoiling our day out for Mam and Brian.

What's struck me is how much like a kid Robert seems, with Mam asking him how he is, and him looking so shaky and white. I'm allowed to go off by myself to check out the newsagents and it's like Robert's the one who has to be kept a close eye on.

Some time after leaving Forton Services, the tower becomes visible. Across miles of flat green fields we can see it looming in the distance, right at the edge of the country. This gets us excited again and we start talking once more about what we're going to do all day. The Chamber of Horrors and the dodgems. Fish and chips and fruit machines. Polaroids of monsters and all of us by the sea.

The car still stinks inside. Even though Brian had a go with serviettes and a bottle of fizzy water from the service-station shop. The sick smell still hangs around, fudgey and sweet. We thunder along with all our windows open, the fast cold air streaming in and rattling the comics we're too excited to read anymore. No one mentions the sicky smell, though. Even becoming aware of it, thinking about it, can make you feel ill. As Mam says, we don't want any more accidents today.

The music all the way has been Brian and Mam's. *The Visitors* by Abba and the Electric Light Orchestra's *Out of the Blue*.

Now Robert is feeling around in the many pockets of his green army jacket. (He's really proud of this jacket. He bought it in a genuine Army and Navy

Store and somehow managed to avoid getting any spew on it whatsoever.) He finds a cassette tape. I'm amazed, because he's leaning forward and offering it to Brian. He's made a compilation of his favourite early Bowie songs and he's asking Brian to play it over the quadraphonic speakers. It would never occur to me to do that. Robert makes it look easy. I'd never tap Brian on the shoulder as he drives at sixty miles per hour and say, 'Can you put this on next?'

Brian slides it into the machine in the dashboard. There's the crackle of a home-recorded tape – all dusty and glittery – and then Bowie comes on, with tinkling piano and his mocking, nasal voice. His lyrics are teasing and snarling. I look across and Brian's got his elbow resting on the open window and he's tapping his fingers in time to *Oh! You Pretty Things!*

After a while, Mam says to Brian, 'This is music more from our generation, isn't it? From years ago? The lad's got good taste, hasn't he? Most of them listen to rubbish. Whatever pop is in the charts. But this is proper music, isn't it? He listens to proper records.'

Robert seems unconcerned at overhearing this. He's looking out of his window at the approaching suburbs of Blackpool. To me the houses and buildings look like those you'd see just anywhere. But imagine if Blackpool was your own town. How great would that be? Living in a town that other people come to as a special treat. A town where you take for granted such things as the Pleasure Beach, the Golden Mile, and the exhibition based on The Show.

Robert is staring at the tall, Frenchy-looking tower as it grows ever larger. And I am stinging with jealousy. Mam and Brian admiring his musical taste. Him being so cool that he doesn't even take any notice of their admiration. Suddenly I feel like a little kid. If I had made a tape for the journey, what would it have been? The soundtrack from an episode from Last Season? 'Get that off! What's that? It's just noise and shouting!' Or *Geoff Love and his Orchestra Play Space Themes*. Or Angela Lansbury on my Disney record, singing, 'Bobbing along, bobbing along . . . on the bottom of the beautiful briny sea . . .'

I'd never say it to Robert Woolf, but that's still my favourite song ever.

Mam always tells the story of how, when I was five, I was obsessed with the film that song comes from, the part-cartoon, part-live action *Bedknobs and Broomsticks*. Whenever we had company at our house – aunties, uncles, Big and Little Nannas – I would ask for the record and make everyone sing along. Everyone would have to get their feet up off the carpet – the blue swirly carpet – which was, of course, the beautiful briny sea. We were all in danger of drowning or being chomped by sharks. My dad had smuggled me into Darlington Odeon to see *Jaws* with him when I was five. So I knew exactly what danger lurked at the bottom of the sea.

It seems daft now, the thought of all those adults taking any notice of me and doing what I said. 'Get your feet up! Here come the sharks! Start the record, Mam! Everyone sing! Altogether now!'

I can remember doing that. I can remember being that kid. The kid who would show off for the whole room, telling everyone what to do.

'That's just like your Little Nanna,' Mam says. 'She'd show off for everyone. You used to be more like that side of the family. Braggards and gobshites, they are.'

But I'm not like that now, am I? Now I'd balk at tapping Brian on the shoulder, or asking him to play a tape I'd made. When did I go quiet? When did I turn into this person? Timid and shy, and wanting to sit in the corner whenever there's a crowd or a gathering of any sort. What happened to make me like this?

I can hear my own voice, perfectly crisp and clear in my head. But Mam says I mumble too much when I talk to other people. When I ask for things in shops I tend to gabble, and run my words together too fast.

I just want to get the sentences out quickly, and out they come in a mumbly rush. 'You have to smile more,' Mam tells me. 'You have to sound more cheerful and confident. That's what people like to see. You mustn't hold yourself back, being shy,' she says, 'like I always have. You never get anywhere then. People take a lend of you. They bully you or rob you or don't even notice you. Don't be like that. Be more confident. Be a happier bairn!'

But it's hard. It feels embarrassing, somehow, and fake, to act all cheery and confident. Like Robert is being right now. He's talking all politely to my parents in our car.

'I much prefer the earlier albums, during the time of *Ziggy Stardust* and *Aladdin Sane*. But then, I also enjoy his more experimental, electronic records that he made in Berlin in the late seventies . . .'

'Oh, yes?' Mam smiles at him, turning round in her seat to talk to him. He's rabbiting on about Bowie. He's being a bit smarmy actually. This is the same Robert who goes about scowling in black denim, with jangling pirate earrings and studded belts. He's talking to my mam like she's not anyone's mam, she's just another person.

And we are sitting in this car that reeks of his sick. It's his foul stomach juices we are breathing in, every minute we spend in this car. Our relatively new car, steeped in vomit. The smell will linger in the upholstery for ever, I just know it and, wherever we go, we'll remember this trip.

Now Mam is saying, 'Our David used to like that song about the goblin – or the gnome! – that Bowie sang. What was it?'

'*The Laughing Gnome*!' Robert says, turning to look at me.

'I didn't!' I protest. 'I hate it!'

I have learned enough from Robert and his sister to know that *The Laughing Gnome* is a silly novelty record that Bowie made before he was even Bowie and that any proper Bowie fan will have nothing to do with it.

'But you loved it!' Mam cries. 'We used to have to play it again and again. You loved all the daft jokes at the end. "'Aven't you got a gnome to go to?"'

Robert's still smirking at me. I know he's thinking – that's the real difference between us, after everything else – that he listens to records like *Ziggy Stardust* and I'm happy with *The Laughing Gnome*.

Suddenly we're off the motorway. The roads leading into Blackpool city centre are chockablock. Brian has to concentrate. Mam turns the volume on the tape deck down. We're looking for a place where we can park the car all afternoon, until midnight and our drive down the Golden Mile, taking in all the illuminations. We need a car park somewhere near the seafront, somewhere near the Central Pier.

We have a fraught time getting there. The drivers in Blackpool are terrible, Brian says. He yells at them all and Mam tries to calm him and hush him up. Robert sits back and enjoys the way Brian shouts at other cars.

Bowie sings *Time* as we go round and round, looking for a spot. It's the last Saturday of the season in the middle of town, so it takes a little while. Robert nudges me hard in the ribs as Bowie sings the bit in his song with the really rude words in. I can't believe Robert's put that song on the tape. I reckon that he's done it on purpose, just so the really rude words would be played over the speakers in our car.

Nobody says anything. I don't know if they're angry about the language, about Bowie, or the shunting and waiting and crawling around, looking for somewhere to park. Robert keeps nudging me as the song plays in the background.

Saturday, late afternoon

Mam and Brian are going to spend an hour round the shops while we go to the exhibition.

'Will an hour be enough to look at everything you want?' Mam asks.

We just don't know. We're standing outside the place right now and the theme tune from The Show is blasting out of speakers somewhere. It's all you can hear along this long stretch of road. Everyone's walking about as if it's a normal thing, having the theme from The Show playing like this.

'We'll wait by the exit at half past five,' Mam tells me. She can see we're itching to queue up and get inside. Even Robert looks keen now. We have gone into that trance that kids go into when something important is in their sights. We're standing outside the *Doctor Who* exhibition and the side of the building is painted with the logo and the legend: COME INSIDE AND MEET THE DALEKS. The entranceway is, of course, a full-sized police box against the wall.

Mam doesn't like the look of it. 'It looks a bit dark and gloomy in there,' she frowns. 'And it's all in the cellar, too. You wouldn't get me down there.' We've already asked her if she wants to come in with us. 'I'd get a migraine! It'll be all noise and flashing lights in there!'

Noise and flashing lights! We can't wait!

As Robert and I step into the police box – we're actually stepping inside a police box! – I wave Mam and Brian on their way to the shops. There's a very bored-looking teenager at the counter, giving out tickets from one of those machines like at the pictures. Imagine being bored, sitting in the TARDIS. With the music playing, and the sounds from down in the cellar.

I grab Robert's arm: can he hear the Dalek shouting? I notice that, far from being all cool about it, his face is lit up orange and green with delight as he turns round at the top of the stairs. A huge grin on his face. Of course he can hear the Dalek yelling. It's right at the bottom of the stairs, waggling its gunstick and its sink plunger. Daring us to be brave enough to descend into the world of The Show.

We hurry down the stairs and start off on the labyrinth of corridors. We know it's all under a very ordinary street, but there's something uncanny about the whole experience. Corridors sweep round and double back and twist and turn and we very quickly lose all sense of direction. At this point in the afternoon the place is almost deserted by other customers and the illusion is all the more complete because of it.

We have been placed in a museum of aliens. We are blissfully lost in a carnival of monsters. Here are the Daleks, shouting at visitors to beware. They move around jerkily on their castors and swivel their eyepieces to focus on us. Here are the Cybermen, looming, silver and tall. Each twist of the corridor brings us to a new display, eerily lit and pulsating with malevolent colour. I'm trying to take my time, examining each exhibit with care: the Terileptils, the Zygons, the Marshmen. Their alien skins glitter with scales, suckers, fins and blisters. They flex claws and antennae and bare their fangs. I want to linger but Robert is always pulling ahead, yelling at me from the next corridor, 'They've got miniature dinosaurs here! And the head of Sutekh from *The Pyramids of Mars*!'

There isn't time to really stare at the monsters. I want to pause and take it all in. All the detail. The magnificence of them. At first they seem much bigger and more impressive than I would ever have imagined. And they are the real, actual things. The exact costumes and masks we have watched on the telly. Here they are, as if imprisoned in some kind of Time Lord temporal trap: these enemies of the Doctor, frozen and snarling behind these flimsy barriers. That's almost a scary thought, and I love it, the very idea that these extraterrestrial beings are alive and glaring at us with fiendish hatred. The flashing lights catch their glassy eyes as we pass by and a shiver goes through me.

I turn to get a glimpse of Robert Woolf, who's

taking pictures with his instamatic. He's leaning in close to get a picture of K9 – the real K9! Robert has gone very quiet for the past few minutes. He's absorbed in this world, like I am. My heart is beating hard and fast and I find I want to say to him: Are you still not bothered about it? Have you still gone off The Show? Look at it all! We're inside it! *We're actually inside The Show right now!*

We move into the largest room. It is the centre-piece of the whole exhibition. This room is a gloomy, cavernous mock-up of the interior of the TARDIS itself. The central column of the control console goes up and down just as it does on The Show when the TARDIS is in flight. The console bleeps and whirrs and lights are blinking and it feels, just for a second, that we really are flying through time and space. The concrete floor, which smells ever so slightly of old carpet and mouldy damp, seems to sway underfoot. We are spinning through the vortex. On our way to new adventures.

'Robert,' I prompt. 'Use my Polaroid.'

I get it all set up, with the clunky flashbulbs set on top of the camera. I want a picture of myself standing by the console. There's a fibre-glass barrier, so I can't actually touch it, or mess with the controls. The flash goes off, brilliant blue-white, and I think I might have been standing too close. My face might be blanked out. I take the camera back off Robert and he wants one taking as well, with him at the helm of the TARDIS, too. I've been pocketing the pictures as we take them, to let them develop as we go on and take others: Robert standing in front of Davros and the Daleks; me beside the Cybermen in their world of tinfoil tombs. Robert takes a picture of me, grinning, with a Zygon in the background.

After a while, Robert starts to get restless. He turns to me and says, 'Mind you, some of them are a bit tatty, aren't they? Look at the holes in that one. You can see the stuffing coming out. And look – the Cyberman's leg is ripped. There's polysterene underneath! You can see! Ha!'

I frown at this. He's laughing in the *Doctor Who* exhibition. For a second it seems as shocking as laughing in church. He laughs at a display of model spaceships that have been used over the years.

'You can see what they're made out of,' he says. 'Washing-up liquid bottles. Shampoo bottles. Bits of Airfix plane kits! Sticky-backed plastic!'

I stare at the fake spaceships and think: But we *know* that! That's the point! Someone's spent hours making them out of very ordinary things. That's what I love about them. I love the fact that stuff in space comes from stuff you'd find in your own kitchen at home.

But Robert has become ruthless. It's like his mood has changed in a matter of minutes. He's suddenly embarrassed about the enthusiasm he let show when we first came in. He laughs, 'Some of it's a bit crap, Davey. A bit of a let-down. You have to admit.'

He's even saying this in the console room, where the lights are flashing so busily, to create the illusion of travelling through time. Where the Cybermen and Daleks are yelling at us in pre-recorded voices. And everything is working full tilt to drag us into the worlds of *Doctor Who*. And here's Robert Woolf, sighing and leaning against the wall, starting to look bored. 'Have we seen everything? Is it time for us to go yet?'

There's a video screen before the stairs to the exit. The new Doctor, Peter Davison, is on it, in a loop, asking us again and again, 'Did you enjoy your visit?' He grins. 'Then come again soon!'

For a moment I'm wondering what Jacqui would have made of it. If she still lived with us – if she hadn't returned to New York City – I bet she would have come down into the exhibition with us.

Now it's darker at half past five, the Central Pier and the Golden Mile look a bit more spectacular. When we step out of the exhibition, it takes a few moments for us to get our bearings and work out which side of the building we are on.

All the lights are flashing now, strung in Christmassy festoons across the busy roads. The traffic has gone mad and crowds are surging along the pavement. There's a lot of noise. A buzz of hilarious excitement. Hard, pale faces are swarming by, wearing silly hats, green fluorescent necklaces, jamming hanks of candyfloss into greedy mouths. The cool air eddies with gusts of hot onions, curry sauce, and the grassy stink of horse muck in the road. The black horse-drawn carriages go jingling by, even more quaintly old-fashioned than the trams. The steamy white windows slide by against the purple dark, sharply tooting as they pause on the Golden Mile.

Me and Robert stand in the lee of the exhibition building. We stare at the Polaroid photos as they develop fully. 'It was fantastic down there, wasn't it?' I grin, urging him to be pleased about it.

I catch him smiling just then. Like me, he has got his bagful of souvenirs from the exhibition shop – a silver bag printed with The Show's neon logo.

There's a busy cafeteria on the ground floor of the exhibition building. As we wait, I'm staring at all the people inside at their formica tables. Most are having fish and chips. Funny to think they're right above the exhibition. And they know it too, because the music's still playing at full blast. There's no ignoring the fact that they're all on top of the fabulous dimension that contains the Daleks, the Cybermen and the Zygons.

Then, just as the sight of everyone squeezing tomato sauce on their chips is starting to make us feel starving, Robert points out that Mam and Brian are here. They are coming over the road towards us, dodging through the traffic and the crowds.

Mam doesn't like the look of the fellas rampaging about with their plastic tumblers of beer. Those blokes are shouting and laughing and wearing huge plastic boobs and wigs of curly green hair under glittering hats. I can see she's thinking, this isn't our kind of place. Why did we even come here? It's horrible.

But she smiles when they get across the road and meet us outside the back of the TARDIS.

'Was it everything you thought it was going to be?' she asks. We're showing her everything we bought in the exhibition shop, digging through silver carrier-bags. Look: a police box money box. 'Did you build it up too much? Were you disappointed?'

'No,' I tell her. 'It was really great.'

'That's good! Did you get pictures?'

'A few,' I say, holding up the wodge of Polaroids. But it's too dark and noisy to show them here. 'They even had a yeti on the way out. The last exhibit was a yeti!'

Mam laughs, hugging me. 'A yeti! Did you hear that, Brian? They even had a yeti on the way out!'

'It was right by the gift shop,' Robert says. 'Davey took a photo. But there wasn't much to see. It looked a bit like an old fur coat standing in a case.'

'But it was still a genuine yeti from The Show,' I tell them, as we start to walk off. 'From 1968. A vintage yeti! An antique yeti!'

'Let's find somewhere to get our tea,' Mam tells us. 'Come on, you two. And I'm glad it was good. I'm glad it was all worth coming to see.'

Sunday

Next day I go running round to his house.

It's the blonde twins from next door who tell me. They come running round ours and say that Robert Woolf is tearing up his entire *Doctor Who* book collection. One at a time. With great aplomb. Like a magician, turning to his next, new trick. Bare-chested, flexing his muscles in his front garden as the sun shines down on Sunday morning. He's picking up one book at a time and showing it to the audience of girls, who hang over the backyard fence. Then he's tearing each precious volume into two pieces and chucking them in the bin.

He's just showing off for the girls, that's what the twins reckon. And that means shedding all of his Target *Doctor Who*s. The twins are giggly and silly as they tell me, as if they've been thrilled by the spectacle of Robert ruining important stuff.

What gets me is that some of those books aren't even his. Some of them are mine, on a lend. Some of the more recent ones he's had piled up in his room. He hasn't even read them yet. He borrowed them off me and just added them to his pile of things to read. Now he doesn't really care. Not any more. This is what the blonde twins say. He is outside his house and he is working out with weights that he got for his birthday. Girls are hanging over the backyard fence, watching. Then he starts ripping stuff up.

'That Julie is there,' one of the twins tells me, as we hurry over to Brackett Close. 'The one that lives near him. She reckons she's kissed him. She reckons that they've done even worse.'

Even worse? My mind boggles. Robert's never told me anything about this Julie, though now I remember that in the summer Karen did. But back then I put the whole thing out of my head. And now what's this twin on about? Robert's doing even worse stuff with Julie? What does she mean by 'even worse'? It sounds like something furtive and weird. Something criminal.

The Doomsday Weapon. The Tomb of the Cybermen. Talons of Weng Chiang. One after the next. Tossed in the bin. *The Horror of Fang Rock. Pyramids of Mars. Deadly Assassin.* The twins say that everyone is clapping. They cheer at each small act of destruction.

So I am going round there. I'll get knacked off my mam if any of my books end up in Robert's pile. If he tears any of mine apart I'll be in such big trouble. But I'm also upset about his books. Because they aren't just his or mine. They are all *ours*. They are our shared books. Our big, shared *Doctor Who* collection. And he is ripping them up. Out of the blue. Just on a whim. Showing off for girls.

And they are only 128 pages long, anyway. Do you have to be all that strong to rip in half a paperback that is only 128 pages long?

He should have just given them to me. If he wasn't bothered. If he'd given up on Terrance Dicks, Malcolm Hulke, Gerry Davis, Ian Marter, David Whitaker. He should have told me. I knew his interest was waning. I knew he wasn't bothered anymore.

He makes me feel stupid because I am still so bothered.

When I get there, full of hell, he laughs at me. And so do the girls hanging off his fence. Especially Julie who he's kissed and done even worse things with. The books are in his bin. A few well-worn pages, ripped from their bindings, are scattered about the flagstones of his yard, raggy-edged.

On one page I even recognise the illustration and where it comes in one of the books – it's a map of the Silurian hibernation bunker deep underground in *The Cave Monsters*, by Malcolm Hulke, which is a proper classic.

As the kids laugh and Robert shakes his head at my stupidity, my paranoia, and my obsession, I fixate on that illustration. It's where the lizard-like Silurians went to sleep, cosy in the warm crust of planet Earth. They wanted to sleep away the centuries until the primordial upheavals and all of evolution had run their perilous course. The Silurians wanted to wake up one day and reclaim their place on Earth, but only in the future, when the changes were over, and everything was better than it seems right now.

NOVEMBER

Monday evening

Now that I'm going to be thirteen pretty soon Mam has decided I'm allowed to stay out of doors a little longer. I'm allowed to play out later now, even after it's gone dark. I can tell she's not completely happy, but she knows she has to start cutting the apron strings. That's the way she put it, when she explained to my Big Nanna. Though Mam's never worn an apron, not to my knowledge.

I know what she means, though.

Really, I don't feel any older, or more grown up. Even being ready to start my second year in the Comp doesn't make me feel much more grown up.

I go out and muck about with my friends on the estate, and it's only *partly* because I want to. I also want to make Mam feel like I'm socialising properly and I'm maturing into a normal person. I'm not becoming a hermit, which is something she's warned me I'll turn into. Sometimes I think it's true, the hours I spend in my bedroom. It's where I'm happiest, though I know it shouldn't be really.

You should get out more. That's what people say

221

when you're looking peaky. When they think you're strange for staying in.

I know Brian has said something to Mam. He's said that when he was a kid you couldn't keep him indoors. He ran about outside and didn't even wear shoes. 'Why does David hang about adults all the time?' he asks Mam. 'You've turned him soft. It's not natural, that. He shouldn't want to come out with us, shopping every Saturday, dogging our heels every day. You'll have him turn out weird and wrong.'

I know Mam looked stung by this. By the criticism of it – but also by the possibility that Brian could be right.

So – get yourself out. Go on. Make friends your own age. Play out more. Get some fresh air.

I've joined Robert Woolf's gang. There's only a few of them. They knock about in the kids' play park in Brackett Close, near the terrace where he lives. There's some girls – including that Julie who he reckons he's going out with now. There's some new kids, recently moved in, a brother and a sister. They live just by the play park and Robert's saying that the boy – Kevin – is his best mate now. Probably because there was a sudden party round there on Sunday night, while his parents were out. I wasn't there because we were visiting my Big Nanna. That's the thing about being in a gang of kids. Things happen so fast and things change overnight. I miss one night out and everyone's got new best friends, or they've done something new. There's been some new drama. It's hard keeping up.

Mostly though, you'd think we don't do much when we hang around in the play park in the evenings. We sit about on the metal sculpture things and the tyre swings and the climbing frames, scratching graffiti in flaky paint. We chat about nothing much. Robert gets his guitar out and he's made up songs about each of the neighbours who live by him:

'New shoes,
Wish I had a pair of
New shoes.'

The bloke he sings this about looks ashamed and hurries on by. The laughter from all of us is ringing in his ears. He's a scruffy bloke, lives in the flats nearby. The Far Eastern woman who lives there too and Robert says is a prostitute, she gets her own song as well. Robert has this knack of seeing just what it is people will be most self-conscious about. And he kind of picks on it. He keeps going on and on.

'New shoes . . .'

Like he keeps going on about sex stuff with me. Sex stuff with girls – and I know he can see it makes me squirm.

One night we're waiting in the rain for the others to come out and play. Even the rain doesn't keep us indoors. It's really teeming down. Maybe the others won't bother. We hang about and watch the rain running off the sloping orange roofs, till the tiles are shining. We listen to the rain drumming like thunder down the plastic gutters. Funny that everything goes garish in the rain. All the colours come up brighter on our estate: the mica in the black brick of our houses. The glossy red of the tarmac. The green and pink of the dog-roses as all the bushes nod and sway in the wind.

We wander to the Burn and sit up in the trees, listening to the creaking and tapping of the rain. Just Robert and me, like it hasn't been for ages. We sit along one thick branch, high above a sheer, severe drop into the icy stream.

'I found this porno mag. I'll have to show you.'

'Oh, yes?' I'm on the alert instantly. He's off on his sex stuff again. These days he's got a real craze on, about sex stuff. It's like a fever or a fad. It's like last year, when I went crazy on *He-Man and the Masters of the Universe* for a week or two, after The Show went off the air. For a little while I even thought it might be better than The Show, which was sacrilege, of course.

Robert's fad seems weird to me, and a little uncomfortable.

He starts talking about the magazine he found, and about the weird willies of some of the men in the pictures. He's laughing about it.

I don't know what he's on about. I blush. Anyway, why is he talking about looking at the blokes? Isn't it the girls, and only the girls, that boys like Robert want to see?

He wants to know about stuff. He asks me things.

'Do you know what it means when lasses talk about "starting" and about "coming on"?'

And I don't. I've heard them say things like that, so they must be true things, but I don't really know what it means.

'Have you spunked up yet, Davey?'

I don't answer.

'Does the end of your willy stand out of the skin when it gets hard?'

And I don't understand what he means at all. I try to cover it up all the time whether it's hard or soft. I hate talking about it.

All the boys at school seem so proud. After games and swimming at school they all come out of the showers and everyone has a look.

'Have you got pubes like I have?' Robert says. 'Mine are coming in thick and black. Loads of 'em.'

At school I try to cover myself with my towel. We have to shower together and there's no hiding. Our PE teacher comes loping through, making sure everyone's getting clean and no one's skipping the showers and going back into school all mucky and sweaty. And it's then that my classmates can see yet again that my willy's vanished almost totally inside of me in shame. They're pointing and shouting and I'm standing there and I feel like I'm turning into a girl, before their very eyes.

They jiggle and wiggle and show themselves off. They yank away my towel and laugh at me. Somehow I thought it would have stopped by now. We're all almost teenagers. But now it's worse.

Tonight I get embarrassed and hard when Robert keeps on asking me questions about all this sex stuff. It's like the whole of my body really tightens in concentration. I almost stop breathing. My skin is raw and alive. We're roosting up in these trees and the rain spits intermittently on the canopy of leaves. It gets so dark we can hardly see the ground below us. It'll be a dangerous job, getting down. My willy's feeling cramped and hot in my days-of-the-week underpants. Robert talks and his voice cracks because lately his voice has been starting to break. That's something else he's ahead in.

I'm way behind them all. Not in classes, of course. But in everything else that's important. I can do all the new maths that gets thrown at us. But it's the algebra of everyday stuff that I find I can't solve. I can't marry up both sides of these sums.

I listen to his voice crackle like the bark on the branch under our joint weight.

I feel ashamed. I'm immature. I'm wrongly made. He could tell everyone we know that I'm growing up wrong. Like it's all my fault. And maybe it is. Maybe there's something I should be doing. Something I've missed. And then I'd grow up into a proper boy.

'That party on Sunday. The one you missed. It was fantastic. We made such a mess of the whole place. There were kids everywhere. In every room. They were getting out the parents' clothes. Dragging everything out. Writing on the walls. Smashing stuff up. Anyway. Julie from round our way was there. That Julie. She took me into one of the bedrooms and that's where we did it.'

I turn to stare at him in the dark. I have to squint. I hate the way he calls her 'that Julie'. As if making himself distant from her. Or as if there's lots of Julies to choose from. Or, as if by doing that to her, it's made her less familiar, less real somehow.

'You did it?'

He shrugs.

'What did you do? I mean, did you, like stick your thing inside of her?' I'm blushing in the dark, even saying this. It makes him laugh.

'Not quite,' he says. 'But she kind of touched me. It was okay. But then she let me touch her. You know.'

'What was it like?'

There's a pause. 'I dunno. Sort of hot and nice. Sort of how you'd expect it to be.'

'Oh. Right.'

He looks across at me. I'm obviously not looking impressed enough. 'Others at the party – you'd know them – well, some of them were definitely going all the way.'

'God,' I say. 'That must have been amazing.'

Then we climb down from the tree and walk up through the Burn and back to his street. The rain's slackening off now and I'm thinking that, hearing all this, I'm glad I wasn't there for that party.

He's saying that they were breaking vinyl records, scraping the needle back and forth over the grooves as they played. They went through kitchen cupboards and fed baked beans into the tropical fish tank. They pushed slices of salami and frozen oven chips into the video recorder.

And suddenly I imagine all of that happening in our house. Mam and Brian away and all the kids I know rushing into our place. I can imagine all that chaos and disaster.

I can see the expression on Mam's face when she finds out. I only have to picture it for a second. Hurt and betrayal. The home she's made and kept nicely for us. Destroyed by kids.

Tonight, now the rain has stopped, the other kids are coming out. Someone's got a radio going in the play park. It's fully dark when we get there. Robert's new best friend isn't coming out, nor is his sister. They're grounded because of the party they held.

Now Robert's doing this thing he often does. Getting a big stick and poking it into gobbets of dog muck he finds on the communal grass. He balances the clod of dog muck for a second, showing off. Everyone laughs and ducks as he threatens to lob it at them. On the radio there's that theme from the movie, *Rocky Three: The Eye of the Tiger*. Robert waves the shite on a stick around in time to the music.

Then he turns and slashes the stick through the air like an ace cricketer. His aim is dead on. The idea is to get the shite to stick to the sides of people's houses. The houses that back onto the play park always get it the worst. It's extra points for getting dog muck to stick to their windows.

But that's it. I've had enough for one night. I get up off the tyre swing.

Robert's putting a lot of energy into chucking the shite about tonight. It's like he's cross at something. Something he can't or won't say. He's all worked up, as Julie and the others watch him and laugh at his new game.

'I'm going in,' I tell them. 'I've got stuff to do.'

And they shrug, because they're not that bothered. I don't tell them I'm going home to do some reading. Maybe get on with my writing.

They don't really notice me heading off home and going in early. I'm not really a full member of the gang.

Later, Monday night

Mam has always said that she can tell what I'm thinking. She says, when you've given birth to someone, after spending all that time with them hanging about inside your own body, then you have some weird kind of telepathic link with them. Mam says she just has to take one look at my face and she can tell what I'm thinking. Especially if I'm feeling guilty because I've done something bad.

The thing is, this actually works. Sometimes it

seems she really *does* know stuff. So it puts you on your best behaviour. Although I'm mostly on good behaviour because I don't want to upset her. When Mam gets upset it's exhausting for everyone. She can make herself ill through being upset. So I try to be good.

When I get home that night it's in time for supper. Brian's got the toastie-maker out again. It's been months since we've all had toasties. Cheese and ham, all sticky and hot on the inside, crispy and shell-like on the outside. We sit down to watch a game show they like, nibbling at corners and blowing on them.

I sit at the far end of the settee. It's chilly enough tonight that we've got the big continental quilt downstairs and over all three of our laps as we watch telly. Mam tells us not to drop crumbs on her quilt. Anyway, all the way through this game show we're watching, and then the start of the detective show after that, I can see that Mam's looking along, and knowing that something's up with me. I'm too quiet. I'm deliberately not saying anything.

I take all our plates and cups to the kitchen and Mam comes after me.

'There's nothing the matter,' I shrug.

'I can read you like a book,' she says. 'There's nothing you can think that I don't know about.'

This makes me blush more than ever these days. I'm sure there are more and more things I think about now that Mam wouldn't really want to know about. And she wouldn't be smiling like now if she really knew them.

'What's happened?' she says.

'Nothing's happened.'

'I know that look. Something's gone on, hasn't it, while you've been playing out?'

'No,' I tell her, and it sounds like a lie.

'You've got yourself into trouble, haven't you?'

'Who?'

'You and your little gang. I know what it's like. Kids hanging around street corners. Always getting into trouble.'

'But we haven't—'

'I remember what it's like. Boring. Nothing to do. You get up to mischief.'

'But I don't!'

'That Robert Woolf. You'll have to watch he doesn't lead you astray. He's a good kid really, though. Come on, then. What's happened?'

'Nothing, Mam, really. Nothing's gone on.'

'What happened to your other friend? That girl, Karen? You don't go round to see her any more.'

I shrug. But it's true, I don't. It's easier to write. I say more when I write.

'Well, you're in earlier than your curfew. Something must have happened.'

'Oh, OK then,' I say. And so I invent something. I do this because I can see it's the only way I'm going to get past this telepathic-Mam-knows-all thing. I pretend that the party at the new kids' house was happening tonight. I pretend that it's tonight their parents are out and those kids let in all our gang to have a raucous party, just to grease in with our special gang.

Mam's staring at me disapprovingly as I mumble out the tale. How they played their parents' new stereo way too loud. How they cracked open the drinks cabinet. How there were kids everywhere, in every room. I tell her that I wasn't happy with it. It looked like the kind of thing that could get out of hand.

'And did it?' Mam's looking stern, but I can see that she wants to smile, really. She's finding it hard to be stern.

'Even Karen was there,' I tell her. Now I'm embellishing things quite a lot. 'And she was dancing round in the living room to The Cure. I've never seen her go on daft like that. She'd been drinking. They had bottles of sweet white wine open.'

'Wine!' Mam says, frowning. 'You didn't have any, did you?'

If I say I didn't it'll harm the story. I just know it'll make it seem too unreal, and myself too much of a goody-goody. I tell her, 'I had a couple of sips. I wasn't sure I liked it. It made me feel funny and swimmy . . .'

'Hmm,' Mam says. She doesn't like drink. My dad used to come in drunk all the time. The moment he went off-duty, he'd go straight down the pub.

'And Karen was dancing about in the middle of their living room. Really wildly, like she was out of control. They had a glass coffee table by the settee—'

'Oh no,' Mam says. She's interested, though, in this story I'm telling. I'm making it up as I go along and I think she's really convinced by it. But what am I going to say? That Karen slipped and fell and cut herself to ribbons while dancing to The Cure? And the party ended in chaos with an ambulance arriving and all the kids running out? Robert and that Julie were upstairs and the last to get out, because they were doing bad stuff and worse in the parents' room upstairs? But I can't make the story overly dramatic. If I make it too action-packed and bloody, Mam will smell a rat.

'She smashed the table. She sort of fell against it. The pane of glass fell through the bamboo frame and just went crash.'

'Did she hurt herself?'

'No, she was okay. She just shoved into it and she leapt back. No one was hurt. But the table was lying there in bits. Smoked-glass bits. Someone turned the music off. And we all stood there looking at it.'

Mam's eyes are wide, listening to this. 'I knew it! I knew something had happened! I could tell!'

'And we all came running out,' I tell her. 'All of us, all at the same time. We knew we'd done something terrible. We didn't even try to fix it up. We left the new kids – the lad and his little sister – standing there, staring at the wreckage. The whole place was in pretty much of a mess anyway, even without the smashed table. But we left them to it. And we all went running home.'

Mam stares at me. My story's finished now and I've run out of details to invent. In my own head I imagine seeing the other kids out in the rain. Seeing Robert and Julie dashing off down Brackett Close. And seeing Karen – who isn't even part of that gang – hurrying away in her pixie boots. Karen the table-smasher.

'I'm proud of you for telling me this,' Mam tells me. 'It's not every boy who would tell his Mam what had gone on. I'm pleased you did.'

'But . . . what about the table, and everything?' I ask her. Now I'm believing it myself, that I was at a party where a table got smashed.

'That's their lookout,' she says. 'You got away and you were very sensible. Mind,' she adds, frowning again, 'Don't you ever, ever, bring a whole load of rotten kids round my house. Okay?'

And then she's back off up the hall to watch the rest of the detective show with Brian.

Dear Karen,

The best thing about novelisations is that, even when you get to the end, there are still a few pages right at the back and they contain lists of all the other titles in the series you might like to read.

I go into my own room and put on the light and pick up a few *Doctor Who* books and I read down the lists of forthcoming titles.

Wouldn't it be great if your life was like a novelisation? And you could look down the list of all those stories and get a glimpse of the kinds of things that will happen in your future? All those adventures still to come?

DECEMBER –
THE WEEK BEFORE
THE LAST WEEK
OF SCHOOL

Friday night

Tonight we're going in a small gang to Darlington Arts Centre. We're going to see Titus Groans playing live.

Robert's very proud of his sister, Alison, playing her violin at a proper, professional gig. They're getting paid and everything, and someone's even said there might be a record company scout attending. Titus Groans are going to perform their entire concept album, *Into the Heart*, as one continuous suite, as Robert puts it.

Karen's dad is driving us into Darlington. There's been sleet and snow and it's gone mushy pink on the motorway.

Tricky, being with Karen tonight. We've had a bit of a fall-out. Well, not quite a fall-out. As close as we ever get to that. Slightly awkward with each other, because we've had difficult words.

It was yesterday at break-time, as the sleet pelted down. We were sheltering under the Foreign Languages corridor, shivering on the spot, soaked through after making our usual circuit of the whole school. Karen started telling me about the sexy novel she was writing last year, with the help of some of her friends. How her friends all dropped out and she continued it alone. Her tropical island sexy story about The Cure and Duran Duran. She laughed, like she had outgrown all of that stuff by now, and I said, 'I know! I read it! It was great!'

And her face fell. 'You read it? How?'

Then I had to explain how Robert lent it to me. To give me something else to read, besides *Doctor Who and the Auton Invasion*. Broaden my horizons, and all that.

Karen looked embarrassed and cross. I could have bitten my own tongue off. How could I have told her like that? She must have felt awful. She looked at me. 'You were laughing at it, weren't you? You and Robert? You were laughing at me.'

'No . . . !'

'I bet you were.' She flicked her wet hair out of her eyes. It's auburn, her hair this winter, crimped and crinkled into a kind of 1920s style. 'I could just kill myself,' she sighed. 'The thought of what I put in that book. And you . . . lads reading it. Lads! You're all the same!'

It was about the worst thing she could have said to me. I watched her turn on the heel of her flat granny shoes and walk away.

So I'm glad tonight's still on, after all that. She might have simply said, 'Let's call it off. Let's stop being friends . . .'

But she hasn't. We're still going in a gang to the arts centre in Darlington to see the band play.

At home tonight we were putting up the tree. It's that close to Christmas. Just a week of school left. Almost a year since I started keeping a diary.

I write as I watch Mam and Brian winding sparkly tinsel around the tree in the living room. They're winding it on so thick it's like a glittery mummy. Mam's even put on Christmas records, to get us all in the festive mood.

What would I think, if Robert was showing my diary around to people? I'd be mortified. I'd want to die, just like Karen does. The thought of that makes me go cold inside.

Mam's worried tonight about me going out. It's Friday and Darlington can be a bit rough, even in the older part of town, where the arts centre sits, at the corner of the park.

It's proper gloomy outside. The estate and Burn Lane are foggy and frozen. It's a fabulous, spooky night. I can't wait until I'm out walking about in it, all dressed up for my night out. I've never felt more like a teenager, striding out by myself on Friday night, to meet friends.

I'm meeting them at the roundabout at the top of the main road, to save me walking all the way to Karen's house. I stand under the street lights and it's snowing again and I watch each passing car for faces I recognise.

On time, her dad's car pulls up. His being a policeman reminds me of my dad. The way he used to drive us around in his car. Karen's dad has that same policeman thing about him. Sort of reassuring.

Karen is sitting in the back, smiling at me as I climb in. Maybe I'm forgiven, after yesterday's difficult scene.

As her dad says hullo he's grimacing at the Bauhaus tape playing on the car stereo.

Karen's in a black dress with tassels and a paisley shawl. Granny glasses and her hair bright red with henna. She seems her normal self. No awkwardness between us.

Robert is sitting with her. A studded collar round his neck, wrist bangles, black lipstick. He's gone Goth for the night. Or perhaps it's for good. And, when I sit beside him, on the far side of Karen, I realise that the two of them are holding hands in the back of the car. I catch my breath in surprise. Are they back together? Robert grins at me and winks as if to answer my unspoken question.

I want to ask, but what about that slack Julie? The one you reckon you did stuff with? But I can't really ask here.

Karen's dad asks me, 'How's your family? Your mam all right? She seems a bit protective of you. She doesn't let you go out much in the evening, eh?'

Earlier tonight I was mortified. Mam phoned Karen's dad to ask him where it was we were meant to be going.

'Er, no . . .' I tell him.

'That's good in a way,' he says. 'You need to be careful like that. Your mam's right. There are some funny people out there. As a copper, you get to see all sorts of funny things.'

He sounds just like my dad used to.

Maybe it was Dad who made Mam so fearful of the world?

When she rang Karen's dad she asked him, what kind of place was the Arts Centre? And he reassured her it was fine; a very respectable, safe kind of place. In fact, he and his wife sometimes went to see blues bands there themselves, and had a drink at the bar. I would be quite safe, he told Mam. He would drop us off at the main entrance of the old Victorian building and pick us up again, when it was all over. There was nothing to worry about.

So that was okay. But I'm miffed that now

everyone thinks my mam's over-protective and that I'm a bit soft.

Once there, because we're friends of the band, we get to watch them setting up. Alison looks magnificent, in one of her Bowiesque creations. We watch them assembling their rather complicated equipment and leads and PA system, and then hoist up the elaborately-painted sheet backdrop at the rear of the stage.

Then we're in the bar area, drinking herbal tea and watching the other friends of the band turn up. Robert looks worried that there might not be a decent turnout. Karen reassures him. 'They'll be all right. You'll see.' We watch the other hardcore Titus Groans fans filter into the bar. They are fourth years, fifth years, even sixth formers at school. Proper teenagers. People who have found their style and their way of being in the world. People who are assured and confident, and here I am with them, in the same bar, in the arts centre. There's Muriel, who's a well-known artist at Woodham Comp. She of the blue frizzy hair and layers of Oxfam clothes. She always carries her art equipment in a tiny, battered suitcase, and she's got it with her tonight. She smells of talcum powder and her face is powdered china-white with the stuff.

Away from school these people seem even more exotic, eclectic . . . *bohemian* to me. I can't take my eyes off them. This raffish, gorgeous crowd. They're like New Romantics off *Top of the Pops*. They're like the dressed-up extras off an Adam Ant video. They are futuristic androids. Wonderful arty archetypes.

They're even getting served with drinks at the bar. Proper drinks, cocktails with fruit and umbrellas in. I sit there agog at all this adult carry-on.

Karen leans over to me. 'It's OK. Robert told me. He told me that it was him who gave you my novel.'

The noise is so fierce I have to ask her to say it again. When she does, I blush.

'Mind,' she goes on. 'It was hardly a novel. Anyway, I understand. And I'm sorry for flaring up at you like that yesterday. I was just, like, massively embarrassed. To think that you had been reading my most secretive . . . and awful writing . . .'

'It wasn't awful . . .'

'Oh, it was! But it was a year ago. I was different then. I dread to think what you thought of it . . .'

What I thought? Why should she care what I think? All I remember is being so impressed that Karen had managed to write so much, to fill a whole thick exercise book like that. And that she had kept the story going. She had managed to bring the characters to life, even if they were doing ludicrous things. I want to explain all of this to Karen. And to go on and say that I loved the fact that the characters in her novel were doing incredible, impossible things.

When I try to say this, she waves it away. She concentrates on her rose-and-raspberry tea for a moment. She smiles at me. 'I'm embarrassed because you're so good, Davey. I mean it. I'm ashamed of what you might think of my . . . rough scribbles. You've got talent, Davey . . .'

I know she's telling me what she really thinks. She honestly believes that this is the truth. I have talent. I can write, she thinks. And Karen doesn't lie.

We watch more people arrive in the bar for the gig. Robert is talking with some of them, looking just as grown up as the older ones, just as cool. He looks dead pleased now that there's a whole big crowd to see his sister and the band. He comes back to us and says, grinning, 'Titus Groans is going to have a proper audience. I can't see anyone who looks like a record company scout yet, though . . .'

We scan the jostling Goths and punks and hippies and college kids. Robert is sipping a pint of lager someone has bought him. You can see how proud he is of his sister, who is away in the dark room with the rest of the band, doing last minute sound-check things and adjusting their costumes. You can see that Robert is gleefully anticipating the day when it'll be him and the band that he'll start up. Having their very own gig here at the arts centre.

Then I'm watching one older lad in particular. One of Alison's friends, from her year at school. He's been around Alison and Robert's house a couple of times when I've been there, when the band rehearsed their concept album. He's an Asian boy, elegant and lanky and the colour of milky coffee. He's intense, but in a kind of ironic way. You can't quite tell what he's thinking. He lives out of town, in one of the posh villages, and comes to our school by special bus. He's not someone I've ever spoken to. I just wouldn't try it. He probably doesn't even notice me.

Everyone else is Gothed-up. I'm in my blue cords. Though I am wearing a silk shirt of my mam's. She lent it to me. 'It's not a girl's thing. Look, the buttons are on the boy's side.' It's printed black and grey with Japanese letters and stuff and feels cool and impossibly glamorous. Taking off my jacket as we sat down, I was nervous. It's the most lovely thing I've ever worn. My Mam urged it on me. 'You have to wear something special. Get noticed.'

And here is the Asian boy, Aafreen, two years above us at school, sitting across the table from me.

He wears a slim-fitting crimson velvet jacket. The shirt underneath is cream and open at the throat. His blue-black hair is parted at the side. He looks like someone from a messed-up, alternative, Darlington version of *Brideshead Revisited*. He's wearing blue eyeshadow and the cigarette he's smoking – nonchalantly – is black and tipped with gold. So relaxed where he is, so elegant.

He's not at all knotted up with worry and wondering like I am, fretting about things . . . What if I fall out with Robert and Karen and her dad won't give me a lift home? What if I'm stuck in Darlington, in the snow tonight? What if I look a fool in this silk shirt and someone asks me, 'What are you doing in your mam's blouse, Davey?' And what if some of the rougher lads from school turn up and come over and start being horrible . . .

But it's okay. None of them are here.

I'm watching Aafreen. Elegant artiness personified. He stubs out his fag and stands up to kiss another boy, who's just arrived. Lightly, quickly, on the lips and they both sit down together, chatting busily, and no one takes any notice of them.

Except me. I turn to Karen, mouth hanging open. 'Did you see that?' I hiss. 'He kissed him.'

She leans in. 'That's Aafreen's boyfriend.'

'He's . . . ? They're . . . ?'

Karen smiles encouragingly. 'Yep. Gay as Christmas.'

'In Darlington? In our town?'

She gives me that gently mocking smile. 'Everywhere they go, in fact.'

I look around for Robert. By rights, he should be as shocked as I am. He's probably scandalized. He'll want to get up and move away to another table. We're at a bar table with puffs. With actual puffs in Darlington.

A voice on the loudspeakers announces that tonight's performance by Titus Groans will start in the main auditorium in precisely five minutes. A tingle of nerves runs through the waiting crowd.

Karen shakes her head at me. 'Don't look so amazed, Davey, man.'

I can't say anything. I feel weird. I feel excited.

As we finish our rose-and-raspberry tea and stand up to join the push and crush heading towards the dark room where the band will perform their entire concept album, I'm feeling great, actually. I feel fantastic in my borrowed silk shirt. I think of my mam helping me blow-dry my hair tonight, sitting in front of her dressing-table mirror. Putting a kind of flick in my hair. 'That's much better. I don't know why I kept you with that little boy's hairstyle for so long,' she smiled. 'Look at you now! With a little flick, a little quiff in your hair.'

We're all shuffling eagerly into the auditorium. You can smell the dry ice, even out here. Someone touches my elbow. I turn and it's Aafreen, smiling at me. 'David, isn't it?' he says. 'You're Robert's friend.'

I nod. His fingers feel hot through the silk.

Aafreen goes on, 'I've seen you in town with Robert before. In WHSmiths. Buying *Doctor Who* books.'

Oh no. My whole insides curdle and cringe with shame. He's going to ridicule me, right here and now. Right when I was feeling in the swing of things for once. He's going to say I'm strange and paranoid and obsessed for being so caught up in The Show. I'm even addicted to the novelisations of The Show. How sad is that?

But Aafreen – wonderful arty sixth-former Aafreen with the velvet jacket and the eyeshadow and the black cigarettes – says to me, 'I love those books. I've read them all again and again. Except for *The Daemons*. You took the last copy of *The Daemons*, when I saw you in WHSmiths that day.'

Doctor Who and the Daemons is my favourite book ever. With the alien devil appearing to a coven under the church in the village where the Doctor, his friends and the villagers are trapped. Best book ever. No contest.

I can hardly believe what he's saying to me. I ask him, 'You read them? *Doctor Who* books?'

'For a while I wouldn't read anything else. Now I read everything. Every kind of novel I can get my hands on. Because I want to write. That's what I do. That's my thing.'

I must sound so stupid, standing there as the others stream past. 'Do you? You write?'

'And I hear you do the same?' he says. 'Karen tells me you write stories.'

I tell him, 'Only daft stuff about time travel and monsters. About *Doctor Who*. And stuff all about my family and how weird they all go on . . .'

Aafreen laughs at this. We're both being pulled along now, into the auditorium. Someone takes our tickets. The band is almost ready. People are taking their seats in the smoky dimness. He leaves go of my elbow and he says to me, 'What else is there, David? What else is there to write about? Other than time travel and the Doctor, and monsters and your family, and everyone else you know?'

About the Author

Paul Magrs was born in Jarrow, Tyne and Wear in 1969. He was educated at Woodham Comprehensive in Newton Aycliffe, County Durham, before attending Lancaster University, where he studied English Literature and Creative Writing. He has written novels for adults, teenagers and children, as well as several original *Doctor Who* novels for the BBC and *Doctor Who* audio dramas for Big Finish Productions. His most recent *Doctor Who* project is the five part audiobook series, *Hornets' Nest*, starring Tom Baker and published by BBC Audio. His most recent novel is *Hell's Belles*, published by Headline. Salt Books have also recently published a collection of his short fiction entitled, *Twelve Stories*. With his partner, Jeremy Hoad, he lives in Manchester, where he teaches on the Creative Writing MA course at Manchester Metropolitan University.